SO-BCL-893

VIRTUAL REALITY MAGICIAN

Written by Dina Anastasio
Cover Illustration by Greg Winters

Based on the teleplay,
"A Dirty Trick" by Robert Hughes

Also based on the teleplay,
"Searching for Tyler Steel"
by Doug Sloan

PRICE STERN SLOAN
Los Angeles

Creative Consultant: Cheryl Saban
TM and © 1994 Saban Entertainment, Inc. & Saban International N.V.
V.R. TROOPERS and all logos, character names, and distinctive
likenesses thereof are trademarks of Saban Entertainment, Inc.,
and Saban International N.V. Used with permission.
Published by Price Stern Sloan, Inc.,
A member of The Putnam & Grosset Group, New York, New York.

Library of Congress Card Catalog Number: 94-68248

ISBN 0-8431-3842-4

First Printing
1 3 5 7 9 10 8 6 4 2

INTRODUCING THE V.R. TROOPERS:

RYAN STEEL

Eighteen-year-old Ryan Steel is the leader of the V.R. TROOPERS. Since the age of nine, Ryan has been training with Grand Master Tao, an expert in teaching discipline, dedication, and spirituality along with the various fighting techniques of karate. Ryan has two burning goals: to become a partner in the dojo and to find his father, Tyler Steel, a physicist and molecular biologist, who disappeared in a freak accident when Ryan was five. Although Tyler Steel has been declared officially dead, Ryan is convinced that his father is still alive—somewhere.

KAITLIN SCOTT

Kaitlin, like Ryan, is in her teens and is also an expert in the martial arts. Kaitlin is strong, athletic, and can keep up with the guys without a problem. She is a hard-hitting photojournalist for a newspaper, the *Underground*, focusing on tough environmental and political issues. She wants to be a reporter to fight Karl Ziktor and the lies he feeds into the media in Cross World City.

J.B. REESE

J.B. is an 18-year-old African American who has been Ryan's best friend since the third grade. They do everything together. J.B. is the group's computer and electronics expert and is as hip as they come. He's highly skilled in the martial arts and his dream is to save enough money to go to college and get a degree in computer engineering.

*F*or once, Kaitlin Scott wasn't thinking about the evil Grimlord. The sun was shimmering. The earth appeared to be clothed in peace. And the evil Grimlord and his army of virtually-real robot mutants seemed worlds away. Kaitlin's mind was on the Tao Dojo's tenth anniversary celebration.

Nearby, her best friends, Ryan Steel and J.B. Reese, were passing out handbills and talking to the crowd that had gathered around them. Kaitlin slipped a handbill into the waving fist of an anxious woman and skated over to them.

5

"Come to the Tao Dojo Tenth Anniversary Celebration," J.B. was saying.

"It's going to be great," Kaitlin added. "There'll be all kinds of martial arts demonstrations . . ."

"By yours truly," J.B. laughed.

"And his friends," Kaitlin continued. "There will be food and entertainment. Wonderful entertainment."

"What kind of entertainment?" J.B. whispered.

"I'm not sure yet. The last I heard, Tao was still trying to decide. But whatever it is, I'm sure it will be wonderful."

"I hope so," J.B. said.

As Kaitlin continued to try and convince the crowd to attend, Ryan skated neatly around the inside of the growing circle of spectators. The pendant around his neck, like the ones worn by Kaitlin and J.B., swung gently back and forth as he moved. Every so often he touched it to see that it was still there. It had become a habit now, like brushing his hair from his eyes, or rubbing his hands together when he was cold. It was the same for them all. Their transformer pendants had become a part of them. Without their virtualizers, the V. R. Troopers would be unable to function in the sinister world of virtual reality.

"Please come," Ryan said as he passed out the remainder of his handbills. "It should be fun."

When the handbills were gone and the crowd had dispersed, Kaitlin, Ryan, and J.B. skated over to a bench and sat down.

"Well?" Ryan asked. "What do you think? Are we gonna get a good crowd for the celebration?"

"We've sure handed out enough flyers," J.B. said.

Kaitlin nodded and looked up at the soft gentle sky. "This is going to be a real party," she said. "*And* great publicity for the dojo. Nothing could spoil it now."

Across town, Karl Ziktor, one of the world's richest and most powerful men, was thinking. Slowly, methodically, he balled up the coffee-smudged flyer that he had been reading a moment before. He tossed it over his head and into the basket behind him. Juliet, his pet lizard, scurried out of the way and hid under his huge leather chair. Without looking, he leaned down, scooped up his scaly friend, and placed her on the desk in front of him. Then he tilted back his chair and closed his eyes.

In his mind he saw a world that was his—a world under the spell of his wealth and power. A world that answered to him and only him.

"So, Juliet," he whispered slowly, pronouncing each syllable carefully, "the V.R. Troopers are planning a little celebration. This just might be the perfect opportunity for me to catch them while their guards are down. They'll be so busy watching the entertainment and demonstrating their skills that they won't be expecting anything."

Ziktor opened his eyes and glanced at the desk. Juliet was gone.

Karl Ziktor shrugged and placed his large, smooth hands over the crystal energy sphere on his desk. A dazzling blue light shone through his long, thin fingers.

"Forces of darkness empower me," he whispered. "Take me back to my virtual reality."

Within seconds, the transformation of Karl Ziktor had begun. And within seconds after that, his evil alter-ego, Grimlord, was standing before his minions in the virtual reality computer world.

"Ahh, my metallic mutants," he announced.

Before him, his army of mutant robots cheered.

"In their human form, none of the V.R. Troopers are any match for you. This time we shall triumph. This time we shall defeat these rodents once and for all."

The mutants raised their robot arms and cheered louder.

"The trick is to keep them mere mortals," Grimlord continued. "We must rid them of their virtual reality power. If we control their virtualizers so that they cannot function in virtual reality, we shall control the V.R. Troopers. And then, when the time is right, we will be able to realize our ultimate plan—to move into reality and conquer the planet. And I'm sure the Troopers are so busy planning the celebration they would appreciate a little help with the entertainment . . . some magical entertainment? Eh, my mutants?"

A roar of approval coursed through the army of mutants as Grimlord rose and strolled amongst them. They bowed and groveled at his feet. They saluted him. The walls of his dungeon reverberated with the echoes of their cheers.

2

CHAPTER

When Kaitlin arrived at the dojo, Tao was standing beside the refreshment table.

"I'm glad you made it," Tao said.

Kaitlin smiled. "I wouldn't dream of missing your big day, Tao," she said. And she meant it. Tao's karate studio and ancient Chinese philosophy had turned her life around. Under his guidance, she had grown stronger and more self-confident, and though she was hesitant to admit it, his foul-tasting mixtures of herbs had made her decidedly healthier.

"I see you've brought your camera," Tao said, indicating the camera that was strapped around Kaitlin's neck.

"I'm doing a feature on the celebration for next week's *Underground*. I'll make sure that you get copies."

Tao thanked her and looked around. "I'm a little worried," he said. "I've hired a magician to perform, but he isn't here yet. Ryan and J.B. tell me not to worry, but I can't help it."

Kaitlin glanced around the room, searching for Ryan and J.B. After a moment she spotted them in a far corner talking to two very attractive young women.

"They were a great help in setting up for the party," Tao assured her.

He pointed toward a lovely origami bird that was hanging from the ceiling. "Ryan made that," he said. "Isn't it wonderful?"

Kaitlin agreed that it was very beautiful indeed. Then she walked across the room.

Ryan and J.B. were too busy trying to impress their companions to notice her. There was an obvious competition going on, as they demonstrated one karate move after another.

"That's called a crescent kick," J.B. was saying proudly. He swung his leg around smoothly. "You should try martial arts. You'd love it."

"And this," Ryan interrupted, "is a round house." He demonstrated the move and grinned.

"Oh brother," Kaitlin groaned, but Ryan and J.B. didn't notice her. J.B. was too busy inviting the girls to one of the classes at the dojo.

"It's fascinating," J.B. said, "and we'll be glad to be of help."

"Or maybe I could arrange a private session," Ryan added.

Sometimes, Kaitlin thought, her fellow Troopers acted more like they were 12 than 18. After a while she couldn't stand it any longer. She cleared her throat once, twice, and when that didn't get their attention, she said, "Excuse me."

J.B. and Ryan turned and smiled at her. "Oh, hi, Kaitlin," J.B. said. " We were just suggesting that these ladies check out the dojo."

"I've been admiring your origami bird, Ryan," Kaitlin said. "I didn't know you could do that."

Ryan shrugged. "My father taught me," he said. "Before he disappeared. He made the most wonderful cranes. I don't think that I'll ever forget them."

Ryan's face clouded for a moment, as he thought about his father. Tyler Steel, a renowned molecular biologist and physicist, had disappeared when Ryan was five, and Ryan was convinced that he was alive, somewhere.

"I think it's time to fill the punch bowl," Kaitlin said pointing toward the table on the other side of the room.

Ryan and J.B. turned and looked toward where she was pointing. Ryan stared for several seconds and then raced over to the table. His dog, Jeb, was so busy lapping the last of the punch from the large crystal bowl that he didn't even hear him coming.

"Well, I'll be," Mayor Rooney said. "And I haven't even had a cup of punch."

"There's plenty more," Ryan assured him, as he yanked Jeb away from the bowl.

"What a disgusting creature," Mrs. Rooney said. "Drinking out of a crystal bowl as if it were his right."

Jeb slunk behind the table, laid down, and looked up sadly at Ryan.

"Well?" Ryan asked.

Jeb whined.

"What do you think you're doing, drinking out of a punch bowl like that?"

"Drinkin' punch, dude. Got a straw?" Jeb said clearly.

Ryan did not find it in the least unusual that his dog Jeb spoke. He was used to it. Ever since the accident in the lab of Professor Hart, the Troopers' friend and mentor, Jeb had been a dog of many words. Now when Ryan reminded him that the punch was meant for humans, not canines, he looked up at his owner with sad, guilty eyes. Then he promptly burped. Jeb might have said more, except at that very moment Tao stepped forward and raised his hands. "OK, everyone, if you could please join us in the next room, our presentation is about to begin."

The crowd followed him through the doorway and into the workout area, and when they had quieted down, the proceedings began. The first order of business was Mayor Rooney, who presented an engraved plaque and a few words of thanks to Tao. Tao seemed embarrassed and a bit distracted as the mayor said, "And so, for ten years of service to the community, I am happy to present Grand Master Tao Chung with this citation proclaiming him an honored citizen of Cross World City."

Kaitlin focused her camera and snapped a picture as Tao accepted the plaque. But as she studied him through her telephoto lens, it was obvious that his mind was elsewhere. He kept glancing at the door, where a strange, sinister-looking man in a tuxedo, top hat, and cape was staring at him with piercing dark eyes. The man was carrying a suitcase on which was emblazoned the name "Lex the Magnificent."

"Thank you, Mayor Rooney," Tao said distractedly.

When the mayor had returned to his seat, Tao nodded to the man by the door and announced that it was time for the entertainment. "May I introduce Lex the Magnificent," he told the waiting audience. "He . . ."

But before he could finish, Lex was there, shaking his hand, and saying "Missing something?" Tao hardly had time to think before the strange-looking Lex held up his watch, then bowed to the audience. As the audience clapped, Tao frowned and took the watch, strapping it back on his wrist as he returned to the audience.

"Thank you, thank you, ladies and gentlemen," Lex the Magnificent said from the stage. "There is nothing like a little magic to brighten up the festivities."

Suddenly out of nowhere, he produced a bouquet of flowers and tossed them into the audience. They came down into the waiting hands of Mrs. Rooney, who clutched them tenderly and said, "Oh, I do love magic shows."

"So do I, Madam, so do I," Lex the Magnificent replied, his dark eyes burning. "But to perform real magic, the kind that matters, I need two assistants. Do I see any volunteers?"

Mrs. Rooney couldn't get to the stage fast enough. She grabbed the mayor by the hand and dragged him forward, until they were standing a mere two feet from Lex the Magnificent.

"Wonderful," the magician said. "And now, if you will, I'd like you each to hold an end of this scarf."

Mr. and Mrs. Rooney each took an end and stood quite still, like well-behaved robots. The scarf stretched between them. After waiting a moment for effect, the magician ran his hand slowly along the scarf, and as he did so, the scarf changed color.

Kaitlin moved closer and snapped another picture.

"Now, Madam," the magician said, "would you please place these two scarves in your pocket." He handed her two scarves and waited as she stuffed them into her breast pocket.

"Perfect," Lex said. "Now, Mayor, will you pull whatever you find out of her sleeve please."

The mayor seemed confused for a moment, but when his wife extended her arm, he seemed to understand. He yanked at her sleeve. He pulled. He tugged. He tried and tried, but nothing happened, except that a small tear appeared in his wife's sleeve.

Out in the audience, Jeb was getting itchy. The mayor was making him uncomfortable.

"This guy needs help," Jeb said to Ryan in a whisper. And before Ryan could stop him, Jeb had jumped onto the stage and was pulling two scarves, and one bra, from the sleeve of the mayor's wife.

"Missing something?" The magician asked, as the audience laughed wildly, and Mrs. Rooney turned a bright red color.

When the mayor's wife had run from the stage, Lex the Magnificent asked for two more volunteers. But this time he did not wait for raised hands. He pointed directly at J.B. and Kaitlin. They shrugged and joined him on the stage.

"Great," Lex said. "Now let me position you for our next trick."

Gently, he placed them side by side and spun them around one time.

"Now, how about you? Missing something?"

J.B. and Kaitlin checked themselves quickly and shook their heads.

"No, nothing," Kaitlin said.

The dark, menacing eyes narrowed and the sinister magician smiled an evil little smile that caused J.B. and Kaitlin to take a step backward. Slowly, the magician moved toward his assistants. His back was to the audience so that they could not see his hands.

Only J.B. and Kaitlin could see what he had taken from them. Only J.B. and Kaitlin could see that he was holding their virtualizing pendants in the palm of his hand.

*K*aitlin's eyes widened as J.B. let out a cry of horror. Then together they rushed toward the magician and aimed a perfect kick at him. The kick connected, and the magician went down.

The audience clapped.

"Brilliant!" shouted a man in the audience. "Bravo, Tao!"

"The best teacher in the world!" someone else said.

Kaitlin swung a second kick, but this time, she connected only with air.

The magician had gone, disappeared, vanished into thin air. Kaitlin and J.B. were left alone on the stage.

The audience jumped to their feet and cheered loudly. Then they settled back down and waited to see what would happen next.

And then, as if from nowhere, Lex the Magnificent reappeared at the back of the room.

"Sorry, my friends," he announced, "but it is now necessary to cut my act short. I shall see you at another time, in another place."

As the audience cheered what they thought to be an act of brilliance, J.B. and Kaitlin leapt from the stage and raced down the aisle toward the door.

Ryan knew his friends well. He knew by the looks on their faces that something was very, very wrong. But what was it?

"Wasn't that a lovely show?" said the woman beside him.

"Is it over?" Jeb asked.

The woman looked down at the floor where Jeb was stretched out. Then stared at Ryan in disbelief.

"Uh, yes," Ryan mumbled. "Well, how do you like that trick?"

"Your dog talks, young man," she said. "Did you know that?"

Ryan grinned and nodded politely.

"Of course I talk," Jeb muttered from below.

The woman jumped to her feet and started to move away. She seemed nervous and agitated.

Ryan gave Jeb a quick little push and touched the woman's arm.

"Don't touch me, young man."

"I can explain this. That's just a little trick of mine."

"I insist that you leave this second! I shall inform the authorities. A talking dog indeed!"

"Please let me explain!" Ryan pleaded. "I'm a ventriloquist, and I've been trying to throw my voice."

"Well, you've done a very good job. You certainly had me convinced. Perhaps you'll be the star attraction the next time there's a celebration."

Ryan thanked her and ran toward the door to see if his friends were anywhere in sight. He spotted them rounding a corner, their heads going right and left as if they were searching for something.

When the two didn't turn back, Ryan knew that something was wrong. His friends would not leave like that, not after all the work they had done. But Ryan decided to stay put with Tao until his friends returned.

The guests dispersed within an hour, happy in the knowledge that they had been well entertained. Tao started cleaning up the dojo, happy the party was a success.

The magician, Ryan thought. It was something about the magician. But what?

Jeb sat beside Ryan for a while, and then he meandered into the other room. All this excitement is stressful, thought the dog, heading over to the punch bowl. He stuck his head in it and licked the sides. But there was not a trace of punch left.

"Man, these so-called proper people certainly do drink a lot," he mumbled between licks.

"It's empty," Ryan said, coming up behind him.

"You're tellin' me!"

"I'm afraid that something is wrong with Kaitlin and J.B. I wonder why they rushed away so fast," said Ryan.

"I was wonderin' the same thing," Jeb said between licks. "They sure split out of here fast. They didn't even bother to say good-bye."

"They didn't say good-bye to me either," Ryan said. "It must have been the magician. Something about the magician . . . but what?"

"That dude was very cool. Did you see the way he made their pendants disappear?"

"Their what?"

"Their pendants. You're tellin' me you didn't catch that sweet little trick? Hey! Maybe that's why they beat it out of here so fast. I thought he'd given them back."

"But he didn't give them back!" Ryan said. "Of course! That's what happened. I'd better go help them. Stay here, Jeb."

"OK, dude," Jeb replied. But Ryan was already gone.

Outside, Kaitlin and J.B. searched high and low for Lex the Magnificent. They had lost him. He was nowhere in sight. Disappeared like a rabbit into a top hat.

Frantically, they raced from corner to corner, until they came to an alley. Kaitlin led the way, running breathlessly through the streets.

They needed those pendants. Without their help and their virtualizers, Kaitlin was afraid that Ryan would never be able to find his lost father—not to mention protect Cross World City from virtual evil.

4

CHAPTER

*R*yan remembered the day that he had learned the secret of his father's disappearance. One day, after many years of no news at all about his father, Ryan had received a telephone call from a strange man.

"I am Professor Hart," the man had said. "And I have a message from your father."

When Ryan heard that, his whole body had gone cold. It had been over ten years since he had heard anything from his father.

He, Kaitlin, and J.B. had gone to the address Professor Hart gave. But when they arrived, there was nothing but a tepee-shaped blue door out in the middle of nowhere. The door was only attached to a frame. There was no house, no building, no anything.

Ryan had turned the knob slowly and pushed the door open. And suddenly there he was, in the middle of a new world. On the other side of the door was a high tech wonderland. Panels of equipment lined the walls. In the center of the room was a console with a computer keyboard and a monitor. Lights flashed. Strange beeps filled the room.

And then a curious voice had greeted him. He swung around, searching for its owner, but there was no one there. The only sign of life was a digital computer image on the wall.

"Professor Hart?" Ryan had said.

"Wow!" J.B. had cried. "He's programmed himself into the machine. We can talk to him like he's really there."

They turned and faced the image, waiting to hear the message.

The image didn't speak.

"You said you had a message from my father," Ryan had said to the image.

"Oh yes. Of course. For a moment I forgot. Please put on the headsets that are in front of you."

The Troopers had placed the headsets over their eyes. In a few seconds the image of Tyler Steel had materialized.

Ryan understood what he was seeing immediately. He was in a virtual reality program.

"Where are you, Dad?" Ryan had asked. But he knew. In virtual reality his father could be anywhere.

And that is when Tyler Steel explained what had happened.

"As you know, Ryan," he said, "before my disappearance I was a molecular biologist and physicist. I was working with the professor. Eventually, we unlocked the secret of inter-reality travel."

"Inter-what?" Kaitlin had asked.

"The process allows images created by a computer in virtual reality to pass from the imaginary world into the real world. You must listen to the professor. He is your friend. An evil break into the real world is in the making."

And then he was gone. Ryan was stunned, moved, and curious all at the same time. The Troopers took off their headsets and waited for the professor to explain further.

"There is an evil creature in the virtual reality world that has gained possession of this technology. As a result, he and his army are able to break through to the real world. Their aim is to take over the world."

"We will stop them," Ryan promised. And it was with that goal in mind that he had spent the past three years.

As he raced down the alley after his friends, Ryan thought about his father. He hadn't seen his computer image since that day. He needed those other two virtualizers as much as he needed the help of Kaitlin and J.B. But it was more than that. He had promised his father that he would stop the evil Grimlord from taking over the world. And without the pendants, the sinister leader and his army of mutants would break into the real world and conquer it.

Ryan skidded to a stop beside Kaitlin and J.B. They were by three men who were emptying trash cans into a dumpster.

"Hey, did you just see a guy in a top hat and cape run by here?" J.B. was asking.

The men dropped their cans and turned. They did not speak. Their eyes burned, and as Ryan, J.B., and Kaitlin watched, they began to transform into . . .

"*Skugs!*" J.B. cried, as the mutant robots descended upon them.

"Watch it!" Ryan cautioned. But his friends weren't listening. Their attention was focused above them, at the top of a nearby building, where a magician's cape flashed.

Within seconds, Ryan saw what they had seen. "You guys handle the skugs," he said. "I'll take care of the magician. Trooper transform!"

Instantaneously, Ryan Steel, 18-year-old, martial–arts expert, transformed into a metal, robotlike, Virtual Reality Trooper. In a flash he was on the rooftop beside the magician, staring down at the top of his tall black hat. But within a second the magician below him had transformed into one of Grimlord's mutant robots and was now eye to eye, visor to visor, in front of him.

"Nice trick, metalhead," Virtual Reality Ryan said. "Very sweet. Now give me back those virtualizers."

The magician/robot laughed softly. "Ha," he said. "Let's see you try and take them."

Without another word, V.R. Ryan began his attack. But the magician was too fast for him, and too . . . magical. As V.R. Ryan raised his weapon, the magician sent a card flying toward his visor. V.R. Ryan brushed it away easily, but there were more where that one came from. Before he could move, he was transported into a magical limbo. Playing cards of all shapes and sizes sailed toward him, bouncing off his armor, exploding against his suit. As the magician's weapons crashed and detonated around him, V.R. Ryan escaped into the reality of light and charged the magician. Ever-ready, the magician lifted his cape, blinding V.R. Ryan, and sending him sailing off the roof to the alley below.

V.R. Ryan landed and lay still. J.B. and Kaitlin were finishing off the final skug. As J.B. made sure that he was secure, Kaitlin ran to V.R. Ryan.

"Are you OK?" she asked.

V.R. Ryan opened his eyes and retroformed. Then he picked himself up slowly and brushed himself off.

"Man, I've never had to battle a robot with magical powers before," he said shakily.

"Any luck with the virtualizers?" J.B. asked.

Ryan shook his head and moved closer to his best friend. He felt terrible. He always felt terrible when he disappointed J.B. They had been friends all their lives, and there was nothing that Ryan wouldn't do for him.

"Sorry, buddy," Ryan said.

"This is bad," Kaitlin said. "How are we going to tell the professor that we let the transformer pendants fall into Grimlord's hands?"

Ryan paced for a few minutes, and then he had an idea. "Maybe the professor can help us," he suggested. "Come on!"

Without looking back, they raced down the alley. Behind them, the skugs were beginning to stir.

*K*aitlin, J.B., and Ryan jumped on their motorcycles and rode to the lab of Professor Hart.

The professor's image was waiting for them on the large screen.

"Something terrible has happened, Professor," Ryan said when he saw the face of his friend.

"You mean the loss of Kaitlin and J.B.'s virtualizers?"

The Troopers glanced at each other and frowned. They were confused, but not as confused as they would have been if they hadn't known Professor Hart so well. His machines seemed to inform him of everything.

35

"How did you know?" J.B. asked.

Professor Hart's weathered face shivered a bit as he explained. "My computers picked up a variation in their sonic frequencies," he explained. "So I knew they had fallen into evil hands."

Kaitlin moved closer to the screen. She was beginning to feel desperate, and she hoped that the professor could help.

"Without our virtualizers, J.B. and I are powerless against Grimlord's invading forces," she said. "We don't know what to do."

Professor Hart's kind face grew grim. "I don't want to worry you," he said. "But I do think you should know what Grimlord has in store for you. If you put on your virtual reality visors, you'll understand his plan."

J.B., Ryan, and Kaitlin took their visors off the table and slid them on. As they watched, bits of images materialized into Grimlord's ultimate scene, causing them to gasp in horror. Buildings toppled, rivers and oceans spilled over their shores, terrible weapons disintegrated thousands of people in seconds. Mass destruction ruined the world, as the delighted Grimlord looked on.

"You see," said the professor. "By stealing your virtualizers, Grimlord has created the perfect opportunity to break through the reality barrier. There will be no stopping his invasion force of war machines and mutant robotic forces."

One by one, the Troopers removed their visors and glanced around at the others. No one said anything for a long time as the images that they had just experienced played in their minds.

J.B. broke the silence. "Ryan can't battle a massive attack across the reality barrier by himself," he said.

"Somehow we've got to get those virtualizers back," Kaitlin added.

Ryan was pacing, and thinking. Eventually he said, "Our big problem is finding the magician, right?"

"Right," J.B. agreed.

Ryan slid his hands into his pockets and faced his friends. "How about this," he said. "If you guys go airborne in Kaitlin's car, you may have a better chance of locating him."

"Great idea," J.B. said excitedly. "We'll use the scanner."

"And then," Ryan continued, "once you spot him, I'll transform and go after the virtualizers."

But Kaitlin was worried. She couldn't help thinking about the last time that Ryan went after the virtualizers. Ryan was strong, and clever, but . . . she wondered how Ryan would react to a few words of caution.

She decided to give it a try. "Ryan," she said. "Please be more careful this time. We know that the magician is full of dirty tricks."

When Ryan said that he appreciated her concern, Kaitlin breathed a sigh of relief. She should have known he'd react that way.

"Don't worry," Ryan said. "I have a few tricks of my own planned for him. What do you say?"

"Let's do it!" Kaitlin answered, without hesitation.

Ryan led his friends toward the door of the lab and shook their hands. "Good luck," he said. "I know you'll find him." But his voice faltered just a bit, just enough to give away the fear that had settled in his stomach. Would they find the magician? And if so, would they find him soon enough to recover the virtualizers—before Grimlord was able to break through the reality barrier and take over the world?

"I'll stay here with the professor until I hear from you," Ryan said as they were leaving. "And remember . . ."

"What?" J.B. asked, turning.

"Nothing much. Except, well, good luck."

When they were gone, Ryan turned to the professor. "What are their chances?" he asked.

The professor frowned. "I'm afraid they aren't very good," he said. "Without the ability to transform into V.R. Troopers, J.B. and Kaitlin will be extremely vulnerable to Grimlord's assaults."

"I shouldn't have sent them," Ryan sighed. "If anything happens . . ." Ryan felt terrible. "I should never, ever, have sent Kaitlin and J.B. out without their virtualizers," he said.

"I wouldn't worry too much." The professor was trying to sound reassuring, but Ryan was still concerned.

"They're very smart, aren't they?"

"Yes, but I'm not sure that anyone, or anything, is smart enough for Grimlord."

Ryan looked up at the image of the professor and waited for him to say something else. When he didn't speak, Ryan said it for him.

"This could be the end of the V.R. Troopers, Professor," he said.

"I'm afraid so, Ryan," the professor agreed. "I'm afraid so."

While Ryan and the professor were discussing the possible demise of the V.R. Troopers, Grimlord was getting ready. Deep in his dungeon in the virtual world, the evil Grimlord was seated before his forces. He did not speak for a long time. Before him, the robots waited, erect and unmoving. Their shiny metal could barely be seen in the dark shadows.

Suddenly Grimlord raised his finger and pointed it, sending a shaft of golden light through the dungeon. The light streaked through the darkness, calling forth the image of the faithful Iceborg.

"Iceborg," Grimlord said. "I want a status report on our current objective."

Iceborg's reply echoed through the dark dungeon. "Two of the Troopers' virtualizers are in our hands. Now we will use them as bait to draw out the third Trooper and render him powerless as well."

The answer pleased Grimlord. "That is an exceptional development. And the magician?

Is he in position?"

"He is," Iceborg replied.

A sinister grin passed over Grimlord's face. "Since he is so good at making things disappear, I have something else that I would like to see removed."

"Just say the word and it will be done," Iceborg said.

"We must distract the Trooper called Ryan. We must keep his mind on something else other than the virtualizers that we have seized from his friends."

"I see you have a plan," Iceborg said.

Grimlord grinned and nodded his head. "And it is a very good plan," he said. "I would like you to tell the magician to get rid of the dog that they call Jeb. That should distract him and allow us to seize his virtualizer."

"Do you mean to have him destroyed?"

"Absolutely not! We may need him. I merely wish for him to disappear for a while. Do you understand, Iceborg?"

"Yes, Your Lordship," Iceborg replied.

Grimlord sat back in his chair and smiled a satisfied smile. In his mind he was picturing his forces as they moved victoriously through the real world.

"It won't be long now," he muttered. "Soon, with the V.R. Troopers out of the way, the forces of my dark reality will immediately invade. In no time, I will control the real world. Prepare for battle."

Grimlord's command brought forth a mighty cheer from the robots. It rang through the chambers of the dungeon. It echoed off the walls. The robots were ready, for now, at last, their ultimate mission seemed imminent.

6
CHAPTER

*K*aitlin and J.B. climbed into Kaitlin's sleek, shiny, red sports car. Kaitlin took the wheel and turned the key.

"The magician could be anywhere," she said to J.B. as the car sped out of town.

"I was just thinking the same thing," J.B. agreed. "But we'll find him. We have to find him, Kaitlin, because, if we don't, well . . ."

J.B. hesitated. It wasn't necessary for him to continue. Kaitlin knew all too well what would happen if they didn't find the magician. Without the magician there would be no virtualizers. And without their virtualizers, there would be no way of stopping Grimlord.

They were out in the country now, speeding along a country road. The sun was shining, and the world seemed calm.

"We *must* find him, J.B.!" Kaitlin shouted over the sound of the wind. "There is no other choice!"

Kaitlin checked the controls and glanced over at J.B. "All set to go airborne?" she asked.

"Strapped in and ready for action, captain."

But for some reason, the car remained on the ground. J.B. glanced over at Kaitlin and waited, but still the car did not rise. Instead, it screeched through a wild lefthand turn and circled back.

"What's up?" J.B. hollered, as his shoulder slammed into the door.

"It's that building!" Kaitlin told him. "The one we saw the other day. The one with the bars on the window."

"Not now, Kaitlin," J.B. cried. "First things first. Let's retrieve the virtualizers, and then we can deal with the building."

"You're right," Kaitlin said, as she sped down the road. "And we have . . . lift off."

Kaitlin leaned forward and pulled the throttle, then sat back as the car lifted away from the road and rose into the air. Outside, the wings expanded and the car climbed higher, then higher still, until it was passing through a cloud.

The countryside spread out and grew smaller. Tractors and trucks became specks. Cattle and sheep disappeared. Houses turned into blobs of color.

"No visual sighting," J.B. said, looking down. "A sighting from this distance will be impossible. Let me try the scanner."

J.B. reached over to the panel in front of him and activated the computer.

"Anything?" Kaitlin asked.

"Negative. Let's check in with the lab. Maybe they have something. Come in, Professor."

J.B. flipped another switch, activating the communication screen. Within seconds, the image of Professor Hart appeared.

"How do things look up there?" the professor asked.

"It's like searching for a needle in a haystack," J.B. admitted. "Any leads down there?"

"The sensors in the lab have been picking up inter-reality activity in sector Q4," said the voice of Professor Hart.

"Roger, Professor," Kaitlin said. "Sector Q4. We're on it."

Kaitlin swung the wheel, taking it to the left, hard. The car banked, then sailed lower and leveled off.

"Moving in," Kaitlin reported. "Right on target."

Far below, one of Grimlord's robots was watching the plane. The plane was familiar to the airbot. He did not hesitate. Within seconds he was in his plane, ascending, trailing behind Kaitlin and J.B.

Inside Grimlord's dungeon, on the other side of the reality barrier, another scene was taking place. Tankbot had a message for the evil Grimlord.

"There has been a sighting, Your Lordship," Tankbot reported.

"Instruct me," Grimlord replied.

"Field units have reported sighting the V.R. Troopers' aerial vehicle. It is moving very close to our break in the reality barrier."

Grimlord leaned back in his chair and smiled. This was good news. If the V.R. Troopers in the sky could only be joined by Ryan Steel, then his own forces could break through and destroy them all.

"An excellent development," Grimlord smiled. "Let them come, like the fly to the spider. Once they've drawn that annoying Mr.

Steel into our trap, shoot them all down. And then they'll see. Yes, that is when our plan will become clear to the world."

"Yes, Your Lordship," Tankbot said, as he backed out of the room. "It shall be done."

Kaitlin and J.B. were so busy studying the ground, that they did not notice the plane behind them.

"It's impossible," Kaitlin was saying. "From three thousand feet it's impossible to make anything out down there."

"Let's try the image enhancer for better detail," J.B. suggested.

"Yes, but hurry, J.B. There's something in the clouds."

J.B. glanced over his shoulder, then turned quickly toward the dashboard computer. "I recognize that plane," he told Kaitlin. "That's one of Grimlord's pilots. But he's holding back. I wonder why."

J.B. fed a code into the computer and waited as a flashing red light appeared within a grid on the screen. "That's *it!*" he cried after a minute. "We've got him!"

"Quick, signal the lab," Kaitlin cried, as she banked to the right and descended into a cloud.

The plane behind her stayed right with her.

J.B. punched in another code and said, "Ryan come in."

"I read you, J.B."

"We've got a lead on the magician, Ryan. Sector Q4, plane 9. Oh, and by the way, we've got a metalhead on our tail. He's waiting for something."

"Probably me." Ryan walked closer to the computer screen in the lab and studied it. "I've located the position," he said. "I'm on my way."

Behind him, the image of Professor Hart was watching. "Be careful Ryan," he said, as Ryan came toward him. "Grimlord's magician is crafty. You'll need more than brute force to overcome him."

"Don't worry, Professor," Ryan said. "I'll fight magic with magic."

Ryan Steel moved backward and clutched his pendant. As he raised it to the sky, he said the words that would allow him to enter the world of virtual reality and stop Grimlords's evil forces.

"Trooper transform," Ryan said. And in a flash, Ryan the V.R. Trooper was transported to the bottom of a grassless valley.

V.R. Ryan noticed the magician immediately, even though he had discarded his top hat and cape somewhere along the way. He was standing above him, high on a hill, and he looked as if he had been waiting.

"Welcome," the magician shouted. "How nice of you to make an appearance at last."

"You're a different . . . uh . . . well . . . shall we say *man* for lack of a better word, without your cape and top hat. If I didn't know you so well by now, I wouldn't have recognized you."

"Clothes do not make the magician. I still have a few tricks in store for you."

Suddenly the sky became dark with storm clouds. Lightning pierced the grayness. Thunder crashed above them, causing V.R. Ryan to glance up. It was a quick glance, but it was long enough for the magician to get to work.

V.R. Ryan's mind was on Kaitlin and J.B. when the first white spear sailed past him.

49

Trooper Ryan turned, ducked, and searched the horizon for the magician, but his rival had vanished. Suddenly, three white spears grazed him. Then three more bounced off him, and another struck the earth at his feet.

Thoughts of his friends, J.B. and Kaitlin, flying high above him through the savage storm, left V.R. Ryan. There was no time for anything but fending off the spears.

"If I were you, Mr. Ryan," the magician called from some unseen place, "I would not worry about your friends. I would worry about yourself."

V.R. Ryan spun around and found that he was looking through steel bars. A cage surrounded him. Black shackles bound his feet. Chains held his arms tightly.

"Now I've got a real magic act to show you," the magician hissed from somewhere behind him.

"I'm not afraid of your hocus pocus," V.R. Ryan replied.

"You will be. Open fire!"

V.R. Ryan struggled against his shackles as he took in the surrounding landscape. High above him, standing on a nearby hill, several battlebots had been awaiting their orders. When they heard the words, *"Open fire,"* they went to work. Raising their weapons, they sent a rain of fire down into the valley and engulfed the cage in a ball of flame.

As the cage melted under the heat of the raging flames, the voice of the magician echoed through the countryside.

"Farewell, Ryan Steel," it said. "Farewell forever. Hahahahahahahahahaha . . ."

It seemed that the magician's laugh would never end. It rolled over the countryside like the wind, even as one of his henchmen examined the smoldering cage.

"There's no trace of him," the henchman announced. "He's vanished."

The laughter came to an abrupt halt. "Impossible!" the magician said.

"Nothing is impossible," said a voice behind him.

The magician spun around and let out an amazed gasp.

V.R. Ryan was rotating up through the earth like a human power drill.

"You can't get rid of me that easily," V.R. Ryan told him.

"How did you do that?"

V.R. Ryan shrugged. "You aren't the only one who can perform tricks," he said. "I have a few tricks of my own. When I heard your order to fire, I turned to my internal computer. I analyzed the geography of the terrain and realized I could tunnel out. I arrived just before the blast occurred. Nice gag, huh?"

But the magician didn't think it was nice at all. He was outraged. "How dare you use a parlor trick like that against me," he cried.

But V.R. Ryan wasn't listening. He was thinking about his friends. The storm was growing more intense, and Kaitlin and J.B. were powerless against the virtual reality forces.

"I want one thing from you," V.R. Ryan declared. "Give me back the virtualizers you stole from my friends."

The magician raised his arms and allowed the two pendants to dangle from his open palm. "You mean these?" he asked.

V.R. Ryan lunged unsuccessfully at the pendants, as the magician danced backward.

"Try and take them from me," the magician chuckled. "You have barely seen what my magical powers have in store for you."

Suddenly the virtualizers disappeared, and a flame appeared in each of the magician's hands. The magician moved closer, taunting V.R. Ryan.

And then, as quickly as the flames appeared, they transformed into roses.

"Abracadabra, my friend," the magician proclaimed. "Presto chango. Nothing up my sleeve." The magician opened his mouth and blew a powerful blue fog at V.R. Ryan. An explosion stormed at V.R. Ryan's right. Another buffeted his left side. A third erupted behind him.

"How did you like that little trick?" the magician asked. "I've got a lot more where that one came from. Would you like me to show you a few?"

"Not particularly," V.R. Ryan replied. "But maybe you'd like to see a few of mine."

"Not quite yet. It's still my turn," said the sinister magician, raising his cane.

From the tip of the cane came a long stream of flame. The flame shot out at V.R. Ryan, but the Trooper was quick. He tumbled. He rolled. He whirled from left to right, dodging the flame that wouldn't die.

"I must leave you now," said the voice of the magician, as V.R. Ryan tumbled to the left. "It is time to join your friends in the storm. And then I have one more thing to do before I return home."

"What's that?" Trooper Ryan asked.

"I must make something disappear. It is something, or should I say *someone*, that matters to you very much, my good friend."

V.R. Ryan leapt to his feet. "You've forgotten something!" he cried. "You've forgotten to witness a few of *my* tricks!" V.R. Ryan got four swift kicks and three direct hits in before the magician disappeared. It felt good, even though he hadn't had time to do much damage.

Trooper Ryan thought about all the people that he cared about. Was the magician referring to J.B., or Kaitlin, or Tao, or the professor? Could he have been referring to his father?

V.R. Ryan sorted through all the people that mattered to him. But it never occurred to him that the magician hadn't been referring to a person at all. It never occurred to V.R. Ryan that it was Jeb that the magician was planning to make disappear.

*I*n a flash, Ryan was back in the lab, standing in front of the computer. The reassuring image of the professor looked down at him.

"Come in, J.B.!" Ryan signaled. "You must land! You must come down immediately!"

"We hear you, Ryan," J.B. signaled back. "What's up?"

Ryan sighed a relieved sigh when he heard his friend's voice. "Is Kaitlin with you?" he asked.

"Of course. She's flying. Why?"

"I'll explain later. But for now, the magician's planning some fancy tricks in the sky, and you're about to be surrounded. How's the storm?"

"Tell him it's wicked!" Kaitlin shouted above the thunder. "Tell him we're on our way down."

"Hurry!" Ryan signaled back. "And be careful."

Ryan sat down and shook his head. J.B. and Kaitlin had not disappeared. The professor was still there. Ryan wondered if Tao was all right.

He called the dojo and waited for Tao to answer. In a few seconds his calm voice said "Hello?"

"It's Ryan, Tao. I'm just wondering how you are."

"I'm fine. Why?"

"I was just wondering. Is everyone else all right?"

Tao hesitated. "I think so," he said. "Although I'm not sure who you are referring to."

"Neither am I, Tao."

"Well, everyone's gone home. There's just me, and Jeb. Wait a minute. . . ."

In a minute Tao was back. "That's funny," he said.

"What's the matter?"

"Well, I can't seem to find Jeb anywhere. He was right here."

Ryan's heart sank as he understood what the magician had meant.

"I'll find him, Tao," Ryan said. But he wasn't sure at all if that was possible.

Kaitlin dropped the red car's nose and spun through the clouds, losing Grimlord's pilot in the process. The clouds broke just above the ground, and she leveled off just in time, skidding onto the country road, slowing just enough to control the car on land.

"Any sign of the magician?" Kaitlin asked J.B. as they sped down the road.

"None. Maybe's he's decided to pay a visit to our friend, Grimlord," J.B. said. "Maybe he's run out of tricks."

"I hope so." Kaitlin glanced out of the window of her speeding car.

Kaitlin pushed harder on the accelerator and headed toward the lab.

Ryan was waiting for them as they came through the portal.

"I'm afraid I lost him," Ryan said. "But more important, I'm afraid that we've lost Jeb."

J.B. and Kaitlin waited for him to explain.

"The magician said something about making someone I love disappear. At first I thought of you two, or the professor. Then I thought he

57

meant my father or Tao. It never occurred to me that he meant Jeb. But he's missing. I should never have lost the magician."

"You didn't lose him," the professor explained. "Jeb was worried about you. Life is a matter of choices, and at that moment, your friend chose to get you out of harm's way. The magician will be found, but you can never be replaced."

"I wonder," Kaitlin said. She was thinking out loud.

The others waited.

"Well, the only way to find Jeb is to find the magician. Remember those pictures that I took at the dojo anniversary celebration?"

"Of course," Ryan said. "The ones with the magician in them."

"I think it's time to develop them, don't you?" Kaitlin was almost out the door before she had finished her sentence.

"There might be something in them," J.B. agreed as he followed her.

They climbed into the red car and raced into town. The streets were packed with shoppers as they maneuvered down the main street toward the newspaper office.

The offices of the *Underground* were bustling. People were racing everywhere as they tried to get the paper out on time.

"I'm taking this film into the darkroom," Kaitlin told them. "Why don't you hang out at my desk and wait for me. It shouldn't take long." She crossed the room and closed the door to the darkroom behind her. Within minutes she was ready to start. She worked for a long time. One by one she dipped pieces of paper into the chemicals and watched as the images developed.

She had almost forgotten the anniversary celebration. It seemed like years ago that the magician had stood on that stage with Mayor Rooney.

A wave of deep sadness washed over her as she held up a picture of Jeb. She wondered where he was, or if she would ever see him again. And she wondered what Jeb would have to say about it all if they ever found him.

When the pictures were developed, Kaitlin stood back and stared at them. The magician appeared to be just as she remembered him. There were no surprises.

But what about that other picture, the one she had taken *before* the celebration? That picture had been taken the day the Troopers went horseback riding out in the countryside.

It was a picture of an old abandoned building. It showed the building close up, and when she studied it, she saw a window with bars.

And behind the bars was a face.

"What *is* that?" she said to herself as she returned to the chemicals.

She blew up the image. Then she blew it up again, and again, and again, until she could make out the blurred face of a man, with a heavy beard, and sad, resigned eyes.

Kaitlin hung up the print and studied it. Then she carried it out into the other room.

"I had to blow it up several times," she told Ryan as she handed him the picture. "It's still really hard to make out anything."

Ryan studied the picture and glanced up at Kaitlin. "This isn't the magician," he said.

"I know."

"That's that strange building," J.B. said. "And that man. I wonder who he is."

CHAPTER 9

*K*aitlin leaned over and examined the picture again. "Look at him there behind those bars. Maybe he's a prisoner."

But J.B. wasn't thinking about the man. He was concentrating on the building. "If we can figure out what that building is, then we'll know if the man is a prisoner."

J.B. pulled his chair closer to Kaitlin's desk and fired up the computer.

"If we can get into the county records file," he said, "then we should be able to get a listing of that building."

"Let's give it a shot," Ryan said, pulling his chair closer.

61

J.B. typed in a command and waited. Then he typed in more information and stared at the screen. After a moment he smiled.

"Here's a map of where we were," he said. "Let's see if we can find it."

As Ryan and Kaitlin watched, J.B. scanned the area. Eventually, he came to a stop on a spot marked on the map.

"There it is!" J.B. whispered excitedly. "Let's cross reference it with the county assessor's database."

J.B. hit a few more keys and waited as the information he was looking for came up on the screen. The others moved their chairs closer and followed along as J.B. read the words on the screen.

"The building is still owned by the government," he said. "It was used in the early seventies to build nuclear weapons. It's been abandoned for twenty years."

"If the building is owned by the government," Kaitlin said, "then the land it sits on must be owned by the government, too."

J.B. accessed another file and leaned toward the screen. He typed in several words and waited. After a moment he said, "All of that land out there is owned by the U.S. government. Several hundred acres."

"Are we allowed to ride out there?" Ryan asked.

"I doubt it. I'd guess it's sort of like an army base."

"But I didn't see any 'No Trespassing' signs," Kaitlin said.

"What was that guy doing in there?" Ryan asked. "I wish we could get a better look at his face."

J.B. turned off the computer. "I'll bet the professor has the right equipment to enhance that photo," he said.

Ryan was on his feet. "Let's check it out then," he said.

They were about to leave the newspaper office when someone called Kaitlin's name.

"It's Woody," Kaitlin said. "Wait for me. I shouldn't be long."

Kaitlin went into the editor's office and looked around for a chair. Every ounce of space was covered with a toy of one kind or another. A huge clown-shaped punching bag bobbed on Woody's desk. Mechanical toys wobbled across the floor. Talking toys, walking toys, dancing toys, and fighting toys babbled and jerked on the chairs and tables. It was as if her editor had wound them all up and then disappeared.

"Woody?" Kaitlin shouted above the din.

"I'm here."

Kaitlin looked everywhere, but she couldn't see him. "Where?"

"Over here. Under the desk."

Kaitlin made her way across the room and stopped in front of the punching bag. She looked down. Woody was seated cross-legged under the desk, winding up a small metal monster.

"How do you like my new toys?" he asked.

"They're, well, interesting."

"I'd ask you to sit down, but I'm working out a problem with my little friends here, and I need all the space I can get."

"That's all right." She didn't bother to ask what the problem was.

"I have an assignment for you, Kaitlin. It's not a rush, so take your time."

"A feature?"

"I guess you'd call it that. It seems that Ziktor is trying to buy up a huge piece of land. It's owned by the United States government, and they're not selling. From what I hear, Ziktor is furious. He's determined to get that land one way or another."

"Is there an abandoned building on that land?" Kaitlin's heart was beating so hard that she could hardly hear herself think.

"In fact, there is. Why, do you know it?"

"I went horseback riding out there. There weren't any 'No Trespassing' signs."

Woody pulled himself out from under the desk and glanced around the room. The toys were beginning to run out of steam.

"I think I've solved my problem," he said. "But as for your problem, well, the best way to go about this article is to visit Ziktor. We know why he wants the land."

Kaitlin didn't know why he wanted the land. "Why does he want it?" she asked.

"He wants land everywhere. He's a megalomaniac. But there's something about the building that really interests him. I wanted to pay a visit out there, but he tried to persuade me not to. Now, that's interesting, don't you think?"

Kaitlin agreed that it was.

"Oh, by the way," Woody added. "How's the article about the dojo celebration?"

"It's almost ready. And I have some very nice pictures."

Woody thanked her and went back to his office full of toys.

J.B. and Ryan were waiting for her when she came out of his office.

"Anything important?" Ryan asked.

Kaitlin nodded. "I'll tell you all about it on the way to the lab," she said. "But let's hurry."

*T*he professor was expecting them. His wise, 70-year-old face was watching them carefully.

"We need your help," Ryan told him.

"I know. I've been monitoring your movements."

"We've got to enhance this photo," Kaitlin explained.

"Try that computer over there." The professor was nodding toward a machine in the corner.

J.B. rushed to the computer and fed the photo into it. Suddenly the photograph appeared on a screen in front of him. Ryan and Kaitlin pulled up chairs and watched over his shoulder.

"What's the command, Professor?" J.B. asked.

"Try 'Enlarge.' "

J.B. entered the command and watched as the picture on the screen stretched out like a fun house mirror. The photo was now unreadable.

"I don't think that's quite right, Professor," J.B. said. "Any other ideas?"

"Try this," the professor suggested. " 'Run photo image.' "

J.B. typed it in and sat back. This time the image clarified.

"It's working," Ryan said.

The professor seemed pleased with himself. "Of course. I knew it would. Is anything recognizable yet?" he asked.

"Can you make the guy's face clearer?" Ryan asked J.B.

J.B. leaned over the controls and got to work. Slowly, the image on the screen became clearer, then clearer still.

"Well, at least we have a face to work with," he said.

"He's beginning to look familiar to me," Ryan said nervously. "How about you guys?"

J.B. sat back and stared at the screen. "I feel like I've seen him before, too."

"He looks vaguely familiar," Kaitlin agreed. "But I can't think where I've seen him."

"I don't think you have seen him before, Kaitlin," Ryan said softly.

Kaitlin studied Ryan's face and waited for him to explain. When he didn't, she asked, "What do you mean?"

"I don't think J.B.'s seen him either. I'm not sure . . ." He sat closer and peered at the face on the screen for a long time. "I don't know. But I think maybe all you've seen is photographs of him."

J.B. and Kaitlin looked at each other and shrugged. They had no idea what Ryan was talking about.

"Can we get rid of the beard, Professor?" Ryan asked.

"I don't see why not. Try 'Command Shift FH,' J.B."

J.B. typed in the command, then watched as the beard on the prisoner grew several feet longer.

"Wait a minute," the Professor said. "It's 'Command Shift RFH.' "

This time, when J.B. hit the keys, the beard disappeared.

No one said anything as they studied the image on the screen. But they were all thinking the same thing. They had seen this image before.

"You're right, Ryan," Kaitlin said. "I've only seen photographs of him."

"Me too," J.B. said. "But I wish I'd met him. He was a wonderful man."

"He sure was," Ryan agreed. He moved closer to the screen and touched it. Then he turned to his fellow Troopers and said, "That's my father, you guys."

Ryan looked up at the image of Professor Hart. "You recognized him right away, didn't you?" he said.

"I've known him all my life, Ryan."

"Why didn't you say something?" Ryan wasn't angry, or even annoyed. He was just a little bit curious.

"I thought you should figure it out for yourself. I thought you needed to take it slowly. I thought you needed a little time."

"I have to get him out of there, Professor."

"I know that," Professor Hart said. "And I will help you in any way I can."

"I wonder how long he's been there," Kaitlin said.

"I don't think he's been there long," the professor said. "I tracked him in Grimlord's zone not long ago, and I've had other news from other places. I haven't reported this to you, Ryan, because he had always been moved before I had the chance."

"But this time," Ryan said, "I know where he is, and I'm going to set him free. I mean it, Professor."

"I believe you, Ryan."

*L*ook," Ryan continued. "I have to go back to that place now. He needs me."

J.B. pushed back his chair and looked up at his friend. "These computer programs aren't always right," he said. "That's a digital estimate of what that guy looks like."

"I think what J.B.'s trying to say is, we don't want you to get your hopes up and be disappointed," Kaitlin added.

But Ryan was determined to find out the truth.

Suddenly a long piercing siren tore through the lab.

"What's going on, Professor?" Ryan asked.

"It's Grimlord. He's placing a virtual artillery silo on line to blast another hole in the reality barrier."

73

"More of Grimlord's thugs," J.B. sighed. "They're multiplying. We've got to stop them."

"We've got to get our virtualizers back. There's no time to spare," Kaitlin added.

But Ryan was thinking about his father. If his father was in that building, he had to rescue him . . . now. And what about Jeb? Could Jeb be a prisoner in that building too?

How could he help either one of them without the aid of his friends? And how could they help him without their virtualizers?

"I've got to get to that building," Ryan said.

"We'll go with you," Kaitlin and J.B. told him.

Ryan shook his head. "No good. That whole area is crawling with Grimlord's forces by now, and you're defenseless."

"Then we'll get into the building," J.B. suggested, "while you go after the virtualizers."

Ryan thought for a minute. "It might work. But remember, more and more of those metalheads have broken through, and you two haven't got a chance without those virtualizers."

"We'll take the car again," Kaitlin said. "It might come in handy if we have to get lost in the clouds again."

Ryan touched the image on the screen one last time before he retrieved the photograph and put it in his pocket. Then he disappeared through the portal and followed his fellow troopers to the car.

The car accelerated within seconds and sped out of town. The countryside seemed ominously quiet, as if it was waiting for something. There were no animals in sight: no horses, no cattle, no rabbits.

"What's going on?" J.B. whispered. It was as if he was afraid to speak for fear of disturbing whatever it was that was hiding.

"Grimlord's forces are everywhere," Ryan answered. "I can feel it. And the animals must be able to feel it too."

"This is catastrophic," Kaitlin said under her breath. "There's nothing we can do without our virtualizers."

When she came to the crossroad, she screeched the car to the left and pushed her foot down harder. No one spoke. They were watching the trees and the gullies for signs of robots.

"We've got to find that magician," Ryan said as they sped around a curve and slammed over a hill.

"How?" J.B. asked.

"He's here," Ryan said. "I know he is. He pulled a vanishing act on the animals, or else they are hiding. Either way, things are not as they should be."

Kaitlin skidded around another corner and came to a stop in front of the building.

"I have to go in," Ryan said, as he climbed out of the car. "Just for a moment."

But he didn't have a moment. From behind a tree came a familiar voice. "Looking for someone?" asked the magician.

Ryan swung around and faced his rival. The magician was dangling the virtualizers in front of him and grinning a sinister little grin. "Ready for another trick?" he chuckled.

"Quick," Ryan whispered to the others, "there are probably more where this one came from. Go airborne while I keep him busy."

Kaitlin slammed her foot down and accelerated, as Ryan clutched his pendant and said, "Trooper transform."

The magician was ready. "You haven't got a chance, V.R. Trooper," he hissed. "You're surrounded."

V.R. Ryan studied the terrain. Grimlord's thugs were everywhere.

"What have you done with the animals? And my dog? Where is my dog?"

The magician laughed an evil laugh and pointed to the sky. "I see you haven't noticed," he said.

"Noticed what?" V.R. Ryan said.

"Listen."

V.R. Ryan listened. The only sound that could be heard was the noise made by Kaitlin's car as it rose into the sky and disappeared into the clouds. After a moment the noise faded and an ominous silence settled over the countryside.

"What have you done with them?" V.R. Ryan repeated.

"Done, Trooper Ryan? I have done nothing."

"What have you done with the birds!" V.R. Ryan asked, taking a step forward.

"They are waiting, Trooper," the magician said. "They are waiting for another time."

"Like my father?"

The magician chuckled again. "Perhaps," he said. "And perhaps you would like to see another trick."

But V.R. Ryan wasn't interested in seeing any more tricks. He was much more interested in performing a few. He spun to his left, then disappeared, then appeared again, behind the magician.

But the magician was quick. In a flash, his deadly cane appeared, emitting terrifying streams of flame that could be seen for miles.

High above, J.B. was watching. "I'm seeing flashes of fire down there," he said. "Ryan may be in trouble."

"I think we've got some trouble of our own. Check it out."

J.B. swung around and looked behind them. Two of Grimlord's mutant robots were hot on their tail.

"Great," he said. "Now what are we going to do? We can't transform."

"Looks like I'll have to do some fancy flying to keep them off our tail."

Kaitlin swung the wheel hard and banked the car. The flying 'bots stayed right with them, never leaving their tail.

"Dive!" J.B. shouted.

Kaitlin lowered the nose and spun downward, losing the pursuing robots. But there were more where those came from. An airbot landed on a ridge beside several tankbots and pointed to the sky.

"You have them in your sights," he barked.

The tankbot sighted the car, and thundered out his orders.

"Open fire!"

Suddenly the countryside exploded with the sound of tanks firing. Bombs burst around the red car, and Kaitlin activated the throttle and climbed.

"We're drawing ground fire," J.B. shouted over the sound of the explosions.

"I'll try to get us out of their range."

The red car maneuvered upward through clouds of smoke, rocked by the blasts.

"We'd better keep moving," J.B. shouted. "We've lost the tankbots, but those airbots are back again. They're right behind us."

"I hope Ryan is having better luck than we are," Kaitlin said.

At that very moment, V.R. Ryan was afraid his luck was running out. The magician was waving his wand, and before V.R. Ryan could get out of the way, the wand had become a spear and was heading right for him.

"Let's see how quick you are on your feet," the magician chortled.

V.R. Ryan dodged the spear and batted it away. But there was another one, and another and another. He eluded them neatly, caught the last one and leveled it at the magician.

The magician was quick. Too quick. Like a spark, he disappeared. Then suddenly he reappeared directly behind V.R. Ryan.

"Over here," he giggled. "No, over here. Ha, ha. Not quick enough? How about a little black magic?"

V.R. Ryan blinked, then blinked again. He was in a black limbo. He raised the spear and aimed it straight at the magician, but the lance passed right through his slippery rival.

"Missing something?" the magician laughed. "Like me, maybe?"

The magician raised his leg and swung it toward V.R. Ryan, but the Trooper ducked just in time. And then it was his turn. A crescent kick knocked the magician to his knees.

"How do you like *that* trick?" V.R. Ryan asked. "Or *this* one?" A second blow laid the magician flat.

High above them, the sky was reeling from a barrage of explosions. Kaitlin and J.B. were hanging on for dear life.

"These 'bots are right on top of us!" J.B. shouted.

Kaitlin spun the wheel. "Hold on tight," she said. "I'm going to double back on them."

Kaitlin and J.B. leaned into the turn as the red car did a 180 and leveled off.

J.B. stiffened as he took in the view. "Look out, Kaitlin!" he cried. "Two airbots straight ahead."

But Kaitlin knew exactly what she was doing. "That's right where I want them!" she said.

Suddenly the red car collided with the airbot. The airbot spun, then fell through the sky, and hit the ground with a terrible explosion.

"Collision imminent!" the second airbot announced through his transmitter. "Returning to base."

The 'bot swung around in a half circle and headed for home.

"Way to go, Kaitlin!" J.B. said, as the red car cruised into safety. "That's what I call flying."

"That's what I call luck!" Kaitlin said. "I'm looking for a clearing where I can set down. We promised Ryan we'd see if that is his father behind those bars."

Kaitlin brought the car down and landed it neatly in front of the mysterious building.

12

CHAPTER

*I*n his lavish, leather office, Karl Ziktor was stroking his pet lizard and staring at his computer monitor.

"You see that, Juliet," he said softly. "Ryan Steel's nosy friends are snooping around my reactor facility. Curiosity can be a very dangerous thing."

Ziktor placed Juliet gently on the thick wool rug and pushed the buzzer on his desk.

"Get me the mayor!" he barked, when one of his many secretaries answered.

"Right away, sir."

In a second, the mayor's voice shot through the box beside Ziktor.

"You wanted me, sir?" Mayor Rooney quivered.

"I certainly do want you. Get over here . . . immediately!"

Ten minutes later, the mayor was fidgeting nervously in front of Ziktor's mammoth desk.

Without thinking, he leaned over and touched the glowing, round energy sphere on the desk.

It was a mistake.

"Don't touch that!" Ziktor cried.

Mayor Rooney jerked backward so suddenly that the contents of a glass of red soda beside the sphere flew everywhere. Desperately, Rooney mopped at the liquid, spreading it further.

"I'm sorry sir!" Rooney cried, horrified at the red liquid that was covering his hands. "I didn't mean to!"

Ziktor jumped to his feet and pushed his face into Rooney's. "You assured me, Mayor," he hissed, "that this site was completely safe. Top secret, you said."

"I'm s—sorry. I thought it was. I don't know what to say. Please, Mr. Ziktor. Tell me how I can fix it. I know. I'll have them arrested."

"No! Leave them to me. I'll make sure they don't get in the way."

Mayor Rooney took two steps backward. "Y—yes sir," he said. "Anything you say."

"I want that land, Mayor!"

"I know you do. And I've tried everything. The government refuses to sell."

Ziktor's eyes narrowed as he glared at the man on the other side of his desk. "I shall have it," he said. "One way or another, I shall have that land. In fact, I shall have all land everywhere. If the government doesn't wish to cooperate, then there are other ways."

"But it is government land," Rooney whispered.

"You don't seem to be listening, Mayor. So I shall repeat. *I always get what I want!*"

"Yes sir. Of course sir. I didn't mean . . ."

"Rooney?"

"Yes sir?"

"Get out of here. Leave! Now! I have business to attend to."

"Of course. Have a nice day, Mr. Ziktor."

The mayor leaned over and offered his hand, but Ziktor's eyes widened in disgust when he saw it. Rooney followed the appalled gaze to his red-stained hand and yanked it back quickly.

"*Get out!*" Ziktor hollered. "Get out of here, Rooney, before I feed you to my lizard."

The mayor slammed the door behind him and let out a long, relieved sigh. He had survived another encounter with the world's greatest megalomaniac . . . until the next time.

On the other side of the door, Ziktor was thinking about his nuclear reactor. It was the perfect tool in his never-ending quest for power and money. He would get rid of those teenagers if it was the last thing he ever did.

Ziktor clasped the energy sphere and whispered, "Forces of darkness, empower me. Take me back to my dark reality."

In a flash, the powerful Karl Ziktor had crossed into virtual reality. Transformed into the evil Grimlord, he addressed his troops.

"I'm sick of hearing about Ryan Steel and his friends," he said. The diabolical look in his eyes was terrifying. "This is taking much too long. Do whatever it takes to eliminate him, but do something. And do it now!"

V.R. Ryan was alone. The magician had disappeared, and the rest of Grimlord's forces were nowhere to be seen.

"There's a new trick up their collective sleeves," V.R. Ryan said to himself. "Any moment now . . ."

"How do you like my disappearing act?" the magician asked from somewhere behind him.

V.R. Ryan swung around. The magician was nowhere in sight.

"Show yourself and fight fair!" V.R. Ryan shouted to his invisible enemy.

Trooper Ryan turned slowly, scanning the fields with his x-ray vision.

"You can't hide from me that easily," he said. "I want those virtualizers."

Suddenly V.R. Ryan's x-ray vision focused on a large boulder in the distance. The shape behind it was clearly that of the magician.

V.R. Ryan poised a spear and hurled it toward the rock, but the magician saw it coming. He caught the spear neatly and raced forward.

"We are tired of playing games with you, Steel," he said.

"What do you mean 'we' ?"

"Just what I said. Take a look around you."

V.R. Ryan turned slowly and studied the trees. Grimlord's mutants were everywhere. Their weapons were poised. The Trooper was surrounded.

The thought of his father behind those bars gave him energy. He had to hurry. This was going on much too long. It was time to finish these metalheads off . . . every single one of them.

V.R. Ryan charged the magician and sent him reeling. They traded blows for several minutes, until the magician fell to his knees.

"Pleading for mercy, metalhead?" V.R. Ryan asked.

The magician scrambled to his feet and faced his opponent. "Never!" he said in a voice of steel.

"Well, what are your mutants waiting for?" V.R. Ryan asked.

"They await my orders. But this is my battle. I don't need help against a puny opponent like you."

"Well, then," V.R. Ryan said. "Let's get rid of them."

V.R. Ryan raised his arm and watched as it glowed electric blue. With one strike, he sent the magician tumbling down the hill. His other arm was now spewing a steady stream of fire, which he pointed toward the woods. As he spun around, the obedient mutants erupted into a forest of sparks and melted into nothingness.

"Good-bye, my tricky friend," V.R. Ryan said to the magician. He pointed the flame downward and watched as his rival exploded in an orange ball of flame.

V.R. Ryan retroformed and hurried to the building where J.B. and Kaitlin were waiting for him.

"That's one less of Grimlord's robots we have to worry about," Ryan said.

"Judging from all those sparks of fire, I'd say there were a lot less robots," J.B. laughed.

"But what about our virtualizers?" Kaitlin asked. "If they were destroyed with him, we'll never transform into V.R. Troopers again."

Ryan smiled. "Mind if I show you a little slight of hand?"

"This is no time for tricks, Ryan," Kaitlin said.

But Ryan ignored her. "Nothing in this hand . . . ta da!" With a flourish, Ryan produced the two missing virtualizers and laughed out loud.

"You got them back!" J.B. cried, his eyes wide with amazement.

"I was able to lift them off the magician just before I sent him to the junk yard," Ryan explained.

"Ryan, you pickpocket," Kaitlin laughed.

Ryan shrugged a little shyly. "The hand is quicker than the eye," he said.

On the other side of the reality barrier, Grimlord was seething with anger. A battered airbot was kneeling before him and whimpering in terror.

"It's not my fault," the airbot was saying. "I promise you, Lordship. We did everything possible. They eluded our rocket fire."

"Everything possible? Everything *possible?* Then tell me, please, how it was *possible* that we have lost practically *all* of our mutants?"

"It was not our fault. They are clever combatants, Your Lordship."

"Silence!" Grimlord ordered. "And stop sniveling. My magician is defeated and you allowed two Troopers in a compact car to outwit you? You're worthless. Take him away."

Two of Grimlord's 'bots moved forward and escorted the airbot away. When they were gone, Enforcer stepped forward and bowed.

"A thousand pardons, Grimlord," Enforcer said.

But Grimlord was not about to surrender. "This battle is far from over," he announced. "In fact, it has just begun."

13

CHAPTER

*A*ny sign of my father or Jeb?" Ryan asked.

J.B. and Kaitlin shook their heads. "I'm sorry," J.B. said. "There wasn't time to look."

Ryan turned and rushed up a hill toward the abandoned building. The other Troopers were right behind him.

"Be careful," Ryan said. "There might be a guard."

They moved quickly, running from tree to tree. No one tried to stop them.

"I don't see anyone," J.B. whispered when they were almost there.

But Ryan was way ahead of him, circling the building. He moved slowly, checking all the windows with bars, but there was no sign of life.

"I don't think he's here, Ryan," J.B. said gently.

Ryan moved closer to a window and peered inside. He wasn't ready to give up. "Maybe we should go in," he said.

J.B. moved around to the front of the building and tried the thick stone door. It wouldn't budge. "This place is like a fortress," he said. "What are we going to do?"

"Stand back!" Ryan moved in front of them and raised his pendant. In a second he had transformed and was pointing a stream of fire at the door.

"We'd better transform too," J.B. told Kaitlin. "We have no idea who or what is on the other side of this prison barrier."

Inside his dungeon, the evil Grimlord was still seething. High on his throne, overlooking his mutants, his voice was tense with anger.

"Those meddlers are too curious for their own good," he announced. "I want an attack launched to keep them busy while we dismantle our operation."

"But what about the prisoner, Your Excellency?" asked a mutant at the back of the pack.

"Move him into our world. He will become a part of our reality."

"And the dog?"

"I'm not sure what I shall do with the dog. Keep him where he is for the moment."

"Yes, Lordship," his subjects replied together.

"And," Grimlord added, "as always, if the opportunity presents itself, I want Steel and the others destroyed."

"Yes, Grimlord!" cried the mutants.

In a flash, the mutants had disappeared. The wicked Grimlord was left alone.

"Just wait till V.R. Ryan and his friends burn that door down," he chuckled to himself. "They'll see. In fact, they are in for the surprise of their lives . . . or what's left of them."

V.R. Ryan stepped back and surveyed the damage. He had cut out a hole in the door that was just big enough to climb through. But he didn't climb through it.

"What's up?" Trooper J.B. asked from behind him.

"We could be walking into an ambush," V.R. Ryan said. "Maybe we shouldn't all go in together. If there's a mutant invasion pending, we should spread out."

"Good idea!" V.R. Kaitlin agreed. "I'll go first."

"Not a chance," V.R. Ryan protested. "I'm the one who started this, and it's my father. I'll go inside while the two of you stay by the windows. If I get into trouble, call the professor. He should be able to track the action inside."

V.R. Ryan stepped through the gaping hole and emerged into a stone courtyard. The courtyard was empty, and there were no sounds anywhere. V.R. Ryan was about to call to the Troopers when a signal notified him that the professor was calling.

"I'm seeing two mutants right behind you," the professor said.

The transformed Ryan swung around and faced his enemies. "Thanks, Professor," he said, as he raised his right foot and came in for the kick. They came back at him just as quickly, but he was ready for them. He rose into the air and bounced off a tree. The bounce took him back to the mutants, and when they realized what had happened, he was right behind him.

"Hey, over here," V.R. Ryan laughed, as he picked them up and spun them around. "Mutant Airlines, cleared for take off!" V.R.

Ryan flung the villains into the air and watched as they sailed away.

"Bombs away!" he shouted, as they exploded on the other side of the courtyard.

Back in the lab, Professor Hart was monitoring Ryan's movements. But the professor was concerned. "There's still one more of them, Trooper Ryan," he said.

V.R. Ryan twirled and faced the next mutant. A kick to the stomach and a punch to the body sent the robot flying. But the 'bot bounced back immediately.

"Careful, Trooper Ryan!" the professor warned. "He's tricky."

Suddenly, the mutant opened his mouth and blew a stream of fire toward his opponent. Trooper Ryan ducked, then ducked again, as explosions went off all around him.

V.R. Ryan raised his foot and kicked the robot in the stomach. He followed with a blow to the head and another to the side. A few seconds later he landed a punch to the body.

The robot dropped, then bounced upright, as the courtyard came alive with a barrage of advancing mutants.

"Either I'm seeing things or this guy brought his whole family along," V.R. Ryan said. "What's going on, Professor?"

In the lab, the professor was trying to figure it out. "It's an optical illusion, Trooper. I'm trying to bring up a program that will counteract it."

Trooper Ryan blinked. But the illusion stayed right with him. The mutants were carrying samurai swords now, and they were relentless. V.R. Ryan could barely fend them off.

"This is out of control, Professor!" V.R. Ryan cried.

Suddenly the mutants' image fanned out in front of V.R. Ryan.

"This is getting really weird, Professor."

"I'm working on it, Trooper Ryan."

"I don't know who to fight. I can't tell who's the real mutant and who's the optical illusion. If a whole army of mutants is going to attack me, I'd better call in J.B. and Kaitlin."

"I've got it on-line, Trooper. It won't be long now."

The next time he spoke, the professor sounded relieved. "You should be able to see the real one soon."

Trooper Ryan stared in front of him. Only one mutant was in the courtyard. The others had vanished.

"I'll take it from here," V.R. Ryan announced. And before the robot could react, V.R. Ryan threw the mutant over his shoulder.

"Good work, Trooper Ryan," Professor Hart said.

Suddenly, V.R. Ryan's hand transformed into a laser weapon. He raised it quickly, and pointed it straight at the mutant.

"Now let's see who's got the hot hand," said V.R. Ryan.

Trooper Ryan lunged forward, attacking the robot, and when he stepped backward, the mutant had disappeared.

"Where'd he go, Professor?"

The professor checked his instruments.

"He's not on any of my scanning grids. He must have retreated."

"I'm going to find my father, Professor."

"Be careful," Professor Hart warned.

CHAPTER 14

While V.R. Ryan had been fending off the mutants, the transformed J.B. and Kaitlin had been battling a few mutants themselves.

"These mutants are multiplying like rabbits," Trooper J.B. said, as he kicked one across a ravine.

"There are zillions of them, Trooper J.B. I wonder why they're all around here?" Trooper Kaitlin said.

Trooper J.B. landed a perfect punch. "Maybe it has to do with Ryan's father," he replied.

"I don't think so. He's safely hidden behind bars." V.R. Kaitlin whirled around and took down three advancing mutants.

"This nuclear reactor is Grimlord's ultimate weapon," V.R. J.B. said.

"Come in, Trooper J.B.," a voice called.

"I hear you, Professor."

"Grimlord has erected a silo on the barrier. It's important that you destroy it."

"But where is it, Professor?"

"I'm still trying to find the exact location, Trooper."

V.R. J.B. walked away from the house while Trooper Kaitlin took on four more mutants.

"I don't see anything, Professor," Trooper J.B. said.

"It's there, somewhere, and we've got to destroy it. Without the silo, this place is no good to them."

A loud explosion snapped V.R. J.B.'s attention back to the house. Suddenly he disappeared, then reappeared beside V.R. Kaitlin.

"What was that?" he shouted.

"Grimlord's mutants are making me dance. They're exploding balls of fire at my feet." Trooper Kaitlin yelled.

"Let's take 'em." Trooper J.B. and V.R. Kaitlin stood face to face with a line of robots.

Trooper Kaitlin was ready. "Let's take them one at a time," she said. "You start at that end, and I'll start at this."

Suddenly there were two lines of mutants, then four, then six.

"What's going on?" V.R. Kaitlin cried.

"Don't worry," said the voice of Professor Hart.

"What do you mean, don't worry?" Trooper J.B. called out. "This army of mutants won't stop growing."

"It's an illusion, J.B. I've just about got it fixed."

V.R. J.B. blinked, and then there were two. "This is more like it," he told Kaitlin. "You take one and I'll take one."

Trooper J.B. drew his sword and lunged at the creature before him. But the monster was too quick for him. In one smooth motion, he threw V.R. J.B. off his feet and onto the ground.

Then before Trooper J.B. could get back on his feet, two cables emerged from the creature's stomach. The mutant began firing lasers at J.B.! One of them found its mark.

"You all right?" V.R. Kaitlin asked, as she battled the other robot.

"I'll survive." Trooper J.B. spun out and drew his laser from its holster. "All right, pal," he hissed. "Let's see what you can do with this."

But the monster zapped him, then zapped him again, and again. And V.R. J.B. couldn't get even one shot off.

Suddenly Trooper J.B. disappeared, then reappeared behind the mutant. As the creature spun around, the Trooper zapped him with his laser. But the mutant ducked. In a flash, the mutant grew a weapon out of its head and blasted away at Trooper J.B.

But V.R. J.B. was ready. He ducked, then leapt into the air, firing back. "Didn't you ever learn that those things were dangerous?" V.R. J.B. jeered.

But the monster did not stop. He moved directly toward V.R. J.B.

"Professor, this guy doesn't give up easily. How do I get rid of him?"

Back in the lab, Professor Hart had been waiting to help. "Your sword will convert into a laser staff, J.B. All you have to do is pull the handle."

Trooper J.B. pulled the handle. In a blink, his sword became a laser staff.

"Man, this is incredible!" he said, moving it expertly. "Right this way, metalmouth!"

V.R. J.B. struck the mutant once, then twice, then thirty times, until he finally fell—and exploded.

"That's the end of them!" V.R. Kaitlin announced, as another explosion did away with her opponent.

"I wonder how Trooper Ryan's doing?"

"Hurry!" Trooper J.B. said. "He may need our help."

In a second, they were inside the abandoned building. But there was no sign of V.R. Ryan.

V.R. Ryan was moving through the building. He moved slowly, stopping at each doorway. He knew which room was his father's, but he wanted to be prepared. If there were any more mutants around, he wanted to find them before they found him.

When he came to a hallway, he stopped and flattened himself against the wall.

There were no sounds at all. No explosions, no gunfire, no sounds of battle.

There was only silence.

"Dad?" V.R. Ryan whispered. But there was no answer.

He slid down the hallway until he came to the door of what he thought was his father's room.

"Dad?" he called again. But still no one answered.

V.R. Ryan looked in the room, but it was empty.

He was about to move further down the hall when he heard the sound of footsteps. They were running toward him.

"Trooper Ryan?" Trooper J.B. shouted. "Where are you?"

V.R. J.B. and V.R. Kaitlin raced into the room and skidded to a stop.

"Did you find him, Trooper?" V.R. Kaitlin asked.

Trooper Ryan shook his head. "I thought it was this room," he said. "But it's not. All the rooms in this place are exactly alike."

"Maybe it's the room next door," Trooper Kaitlin suggested. She could tell that V.R. Ryan was disappointed and she wanted to say something that would make him feel better.

"You're probably right," V.R. Ryan said. "But in a way I'm glad that this isn't the right room."

Trooper J.B. and V.R. Kaitlin seemed puzzled.

"I've been thinking about how I want to greet my father. It's because of him that I can be V.R. Ryan, but I think I want to be my real self when I meet him."

Suddenly, Ryan retroformed. When V.R. J.B. and V.R. Kaitlin looked again, he had returned to his real self.

He headed toward the door. "I'll lead the way," he said. "I'm pretty sure that he's in the next room, and I'd like to see him alone first."

"We'll wait here," Trooper Kaitlin said.

When Ryan was gone, V.R. Kaitlin and Trooper J.B. looked at each other and frowned.

"Do you think he'll be all right?" Trooper J.B. asked.

But V.R. Kaitlin just shrugged. She didn't know if Ryan would be all right. But she did know that her friend had to do this thing on his own.

Suddenly, the sound of an explosion broke the silence.

"It's the mutants!" V.R. J.B. whispered. "And Ryan's retroed."

"We've got to help him!" V.R. Kaitlin rushed through the doorway and ran down the hallway.

Several women in nurse's uniforms had formed a circle around Ryan. V.R. Kaitlin broke through them and stared downward.

Ryan was lying on the floor. He was gazing up at her with a vacant stare.

"Are you all right?" Trooper Kaitlin cried. But Ryan didn't answer.

"We have got to transform him," Trooper J.B. whispered as he knelt down beside her.

"How can we do that?" V.R. Kaitlin whispered back. The strange nurses were watching and trying to listen.

"Who are those women anyway?" Trooper Kaitlin asked.

V.R. J.B. looked around at the gathering crowd of odd-looking nurses. "I have no idea. Maybe this place is a hospital."

"Then why aren't they doing anything for Ryan?"

"Maybe it's a mental hospital," Trooper J.B. suggested.

He turned back to Ryan and shook him. Ryan didn't respond.

"Is he dead?" Kaitlin asked fearfully.

V.R. J.B. shook his head. Ryan was alive, but he certainly wasn't well.

"We must do something," Kaitlin said. She was geting more worried by the second. But the nurses didn't move. They just stood there and watched the scene at their feet.

Suddenly Ryan stirred. He closed his eyes, then opened them again.

"Where am I?" Ryan said weakly.

V.R. Kaitlin and V.R. J.B. leaned closer. "You must transform, Ryan," Trooper Kaitlin whispered in his ear. "You've got to hurry. There's something strange about these nurses."

Ryan closed his eyes again, and when he opened them, the nurses had transformed into robots! They pointed their weapons at the prone Ryan.

"Jump!" Trooper Kaitlin cried.

Trooper J.B. and V.R. Kaitlin jumped to their feet and fired. The mutants turned quickly and fired back. But the V.R. Troopers were too quick for them. They circled around, firing and diverting the attention of the mutants long enough for Ryan to transform.

*T*he V.R. Troopers moved backward until their backs touched the door. "Check to see if there are any more of these metalheads behind us, Trooper J.B.," V.R. Ryan said. "Every time I think they're gone, there they are again. Like magic."

Trooper J.B. backed into the hallway and inspected the musty, damp corridor. It was eerily empty.

"Looks like this is all of them," he reported.

"Then all we have to do is close the door," V.R. Ryan said. He indicated to V.R. Kaitlin that it was time to leave the room. When she was out, he grabbed the door handle and began to close the door.

V.R. Kaitlin touched his suit. "But they can just disappear, Trooper Ryan," she said. "They have the ability to vanish from one place and show up in another. It could be anywhere, like . . ."

V.R. J.B. finished the sentence for her. "They could suddenly become our shadows."

"And appear behind us," V.R. Kaitlin said.

But Trooper Ryan had thought of that. "Not if we send a little present into their room before they have a chance to pull a disappearing act." He pulled out the gift and held it up for the others to inspect.

"That'll do it!" Trooper J.B. agreed.

"They'll be nothing left of those wicked mutants," V.R. Kaitlin added. "But you'd better hurry and give it to them or they'll be gone before you know it."

Without another word, V.R. Ryan pulled the pin on the grenade and tossed it into the room. Then he slammed the door shut and waited for his gift to explode.

"Get out of there!" Professor Hart called. "That grenade was more powerful than you know."

A few seconds later, a blast shook the bars on the windows and echoed through the halls of the abandoned building.

But the Troopers were well hidden. Suddenly a wave of fear passed over V.R. Ryan.

"Professor?" he asked.

"Yes?"

"How powerful was that grenade?"

"It wasn't that powerful, Trooper."

"Thank you, Professor.

V.R. Kaitlin and V.R. J.B. were puzzled. They couldn't understand what V.R. Ryan and the professor were talking about.

"It seemed pretty powerful to me," Trooper J.B. said.

"Trooper Ryan was worried that he might have blasted his father to heaven," the professor explained. "But the explosion was contained within that cell. It sounded worse than it was."

"Let's retroform and try and find my father," V.R. Ryan suggested. But he knew that it was no use. His father would have called him, or helped him, if he had been anywhere in the building.

The Troopers retroformed and separated. They each took a room, but Ryan was the one who found the right one.

It was a cell—and it was empty.

"He's been here!" Ryan called. The others raced into the cell and looked down at the small table in the corner. On the table was a tray of half-eaten food and a steaming cup of coffee.

J.B. indicated the rumpled bed. "I wonder how long he was here."

But Ryan wasn't listening. He was shaking his head and staring at the coffee.

"Too late," he whispered.

"It couldn't be helped," Kaitlin said, sympathetically.

Ryan shook his head slowly. "If only we had hurried. If only we had gotten here a few minutes earlier."

"Look at this, Ryan." J.B. was in the corner, staring at the wall.

Ryan went over and looked over his shoulder. Someone had written a word on the wall in red paint.

"Abracadabra," J.B. whispered.

They all knew what it meant. The magician had been there.

"That's impossible!" Ryan said. "I saw him explode."

"He's a magician," Kaitlin reminded him. "Full of fancy little tricks."

J.B. ran his fingers over the word. "This paint's still wet, Ryan," he said. "It must have been painted a few minutes ago. He hasn't been gone long."

Ryan turned and stared at the bed. Then he walked to it very slowly, and touched the blanket gently.

"My father was here," he said, as he smoothed the covers. "He was sleeping right here, right on this very bed."

He sat down on the bed and put his head in his hands. He sat there like that for several minutes. No one spoke. No one bothered him.

After a while, he raised his head and stood. He glanced at his friends and shrugged. It was time to do something. Sitting there wasn't going to get him anywhere.

And then suddenly something caught his eye. He picked it off the bed and held it up for the others to see.

It was a crane; a beautiful, delicate, origami crane. Once, when he was very young, his father had made him a crane just like it, and now he had made him another.

Clutching the paper bird tenderly, Ryan raced from the cell and out of the building. If only he had been a few minutes earlier! If only he had moved faster! If only.

He raced wildly to the left, then turned and searched the area to the right.

"Dad!" he cried out. "Dad! Dad! Daaaad!"

But there was no answer, except for the echo of his own voice.

"What can we do?" Kaitlin asked when he was gone.

"Nothing. I think the best thing is to just leave him alone. He'll . . ."

A soft shuffling noise behind one of the cell doors stopped him. The door was shut, and when he tried the handle, he realized that it was locked.

J.B. put his ear next to the stone door and listened.

"Can you hear anything?" Kaitlin asked.

"It's a thick door, but, wait, it sounds like somebody's in there."

"Maybe they moved Ryan's father."

"Hello!" J.B. called.

"Get me out of here, dude!" came the answer.

"Jeb?"

"It's me all right, and my stomach needs food. Get a move on."

J.B. turned to Kaitlin and smiled. "But how are we going to get him out?"

"Same way we got into this place. Burn a hole in the door."

Kaitlin went straight to work. In a few seconds there was a gaping hole, and Jeb was bounding through it.

"Boy, am I glad to see you two!" he said. "I thought my number was up. One minute I was happily sleeping at the dojo, and the next minute some dude in a top hat did some abracadabra, and here I was."

"Did you see anybody else?" Kaitlin asked, thinking of Tyler Steel.

"Just mutants. I was too late for Ryan's father, but I know he was here. I heard him. He called to me through the bars."

J.B. and Kaitlin stared at each other. "I'll get Ryan!" Kaitlin whispered. And then she was gone.

They were back in a few minutes.

"Good to see ya, dude," Jeb said. "Got any hamburgers?"

"Soon, Jeb, soon. But what's this about my father? Kaitlin says you heard him."

"He knew who I was. He said hello and he said to tell you he loved you. And then, when I called back to him, he was, well, history."

Ryan sighed and knelt down beside Jeb. "Well, I'm glad you're back. Now how about those hamburgers?"

16

CHAPTER

Karl Ziktor was sitting at his desk when Kaitlin entered the office. His lizard was on the desk in front of him.

"Come in, come in," he said, as he ran his fingers over Juliet's scales.

Kaitlin closed the door behind her and walked over to the desk.

"Have a seat," Ziktor said. He rose to his feet and pulled a large, overstuffed chair closer to his desk.

"I hope you won't mind if I ask you a few questions," Kaitlin said when they were both seated again.

"Not at all. How can I help you?"

Kaitlin took out her notebook and her pen and wrote, "Karl Ziktor—abandoned building????" at the top of the page. When she looked up, Ziktor was staring at the words.

"I'm doing an article for the *Underground*." Kaitlin cupped her hand around the top of the page so that Ziktor couldn't see what she was writing. "And I need some information."

Ziktor smiled and waited.

"The article is about the land that you are trying to buy from the government."

Suddenly Ziktor's smile turned cold. "How did you know about that?"

"Let's just say that I know. I was just wondering what you could tell me about that land. And, more importantly, what can you tell me about that abandoned building?"

"What abandoned building? I don't know anything about an abandoned building."

"Well, there's an old stone building on that land. It was once used as a nuclear reactor, and now it's abandoned. But of course you know all this."

Ziktor shook his head. "What else can you tell me about my land?"

"Your land? Isn't it the government's land . . . at least for now?"

"It'll be mine soon," Ziktor assured her. "But let's get back to this building. Tell me more."

"I don't know any more. My pictures . . . "

"Pictures! You mean, you've been out there taking photographs?"

Suddenly Kaitlin stopped talking. She had been saying too much. Maybe they shouldn't have been on that land at all.

"Well," Ziktor continued, "I shall own that land soon."

"I hear that government inspectors check the reactor every so often."

"Yes, that's the problem," Ziktor mumbled.

"Pardon?"

"Nothing. Nothing. Is there anything else?"

"What are you planning on doing with the land?"

Mine! Ziktor thought. It will be *mine!* But he said something quite different. "I shall make it into a wonderful park, with a playground for the children, and horseback riding trails, and wonderful gardens."

Kaitlin frowned and stood up. "Thank you," she said. "This should do fine."

Kaitlin left the office and headed straight to the dojo. She hurried into the workout area to look for J.B. and Ryan. Ryan was practicing his moves on the mat in the middle of the floor. He had been practicing for three days straight, breaking only for meals and to sleep, and J.B. was getting worried.

J.B. was standing in the corner, watching his friend.

"He's not the same since he missed finding his father," J.B. said.

"I wonder if he blames himself," Kaitlin said.

Ryan raised his left leg and swung around. He was facing them now, but he barely glanced at them.

"We've got to find a way to pull him out of this," Kaitlin sighed. "We've just *got* to."

"Maybe if we get his mind off it. . . ."

They watched Ryan for several minutes before Kaitlin remembered to tell J.B. about her interview with Ziktor.

"There was something very strange about it. He didn't give me much information, but he did say one important thing. He said that he was going to turn that land into a park with playgrounds and gardens."

"Karl Ziktor said *that?*"

"Exactly what I thought. Karl Ziktor has never done anything for anyone but himself. He was obviously lying," said Kaitlin.

"I wonder what he *is* going to do with it?" J.B. said. "That nuclear reactor isn't any good to anyone, unless they're planning on blowing up all of mankind and taking over the world, of course." J.B. laughed. "Which reminds me. Professor Hart called a while ago. He needs us in the lab."

Kaitlin and J.B. glanced at each other and nodded. They were both thinking the same thing. A call from the professor was just what they needed to shift Ryan's attention.

Kaitlin walked over to the mat and waited until Ryan had finished his move. Then she tapped him on the shoulder.

"Professor Hart wants us in the lab," she said.

Ryan's eyes widened. "Maybe he's received word about my father," he said.

Ryan threw on a jacket and led the others out the door. Jeb followed close on their heels. He hadn't let them out of his sight since he'd been rescued.

"Prison is not my thing," he'd said, after he'd finished eating his fourth hamburger. "From now on I'm your shadow. Just make sure you turn around and to check that I'm still there."

The Troopers had promised. They had missed Jeb more than they ever would have guessed.

On the way to the lab, Ryan didn't speak or look at his friends. His mind was on his father.

The professor's image was waiting when they reached the lab.

"Have you heard anything about my father?" Ryan asked anxiously, as they passed into the lab.

"I'm afraid not, Ryan."

Ryan's shoulders slumped. "Oh, I thought, well, maybe . . ."

"I wish I could say that I had located him, but I can't. I'm searching, but they have hidden him well."

"But you called us, Professor," Kaitlin reminded him.

"Oh yes, so I did. Let me try and think why."

"If it didn't have something to do with Ryan's father, maybe there was something about the nuclear reactor. Did you pinpoint the location?"

Professor Hart's image brightened. "Yes! Of course. That was it. I've found the exact location. And there are signs that Grimlord is

122

planning on building a nuclear bomb and taking over the world."

The professor's words shook Ryan back to reality. He listened carefully as Professor Hart explained everything.

"There are signs of life out there."

"My father?" Ryan asked.

"I don't think so. But there are mutants of all shapes and sizes, and they are very busy,"

"Like beavers at work on a dam," Jeb added.

"More like bees in a hive," the professor said. "There seem to be hundreds of them buzzing around out there. But most worrisome of all is the magician."

"Have you found him?" J.B. asked.

"In a way, yes. He is clearly one of the bees. A chief worker bee it appears."

"Maybe my father's disappearance was one of his dirty little tricks," Ryan said angrily.

"Well, he's hard at work out by that silo," the professor said. "And he's got a *big* trick up his sleeve this time."

The Troopers stared at each other and thought about what the professor was saying. If the magician's big trick was to blow up the world, then they'd have to stop him immediately. But how?

"You'll have to destroy that silo," the professor said. "And you'll have to do it fast. Without the silo, they cannot carry out their plan."

*I*m going to find the magician if it's the last thing I do!" Ryan said. "And this time he's going to talk before he explodes. If anyone knows where my father is, it's that slippery little trickster."

"We'll take care of the silo, Ryan," J.B. promised.

"But if you want to get that information out of the magician, you'd better get him out of the way before we destroy it," Kaitlin added.

"Be careful," Professor Hart said. "I'll be watching. And remember, you don't have much time."

The Troopers nodded and disappeared through the portal. When they emerged, they climbed into Kaitlin's red car. But before they had a chance to drive away, Jeb came bounding out of the lab.

"Hey, dudes," he shouted as he jumped up and leapt into the back seat, "What about me?"

"This is dangerous," Ryan told him. "You could get hurt. Why don't you stay in the lab with the professor."

"No way! You know what happened the last time you left me. I vanished into thin air. This time I'm right beside you. Anyway, you guys have all the fun."

"Oh, all right," Ryan agreed. "There's no time to argue with you. But you'll have to hide someplace."

"I like it here. I'm staying right here in this cozy back seat."

The car sped up and headed toward the building.

"There they are!" J.B. cried, as they came over the crest of the hill.

The silo towered before them. It rose up from the ground like a mountain in the desert. But it was a desert filled with creatures—Grimlord's creatures. The silo was surrounded by a whole army of sinister little mutant robots.

Kaitlin skidded to a stop. Then she raised her pendant and waited for the other Troopers to do the same.

"Trooper transform!" they said together, and in a flash they were ready.

V.R. Ryan leapt from the car and raced toward the silo. V.R. J.B. and V.R. Kaitlin watched him run. He bounded across the grass without hesitating. He knew where he was going. He wanted that magician, and he wanted him badly.

"Prepare to go airborne," Trooper Kaitlin said, as she raced the car down the road.

"Prepare to go what?" Jeb hollered from the back seat.

But no one answered him.

"I've changed my mind!" Jeb pleaded. "Take me back! Take me home!"

"Quiet, Jeb!" V.R. Kaitlin said. "You can't get out now, unless you want to parachute out."

Jeb glanced out the window and moaned. "AHHHHHHHHHH!" he said.

"*Wait!*" cautioned the voice of Professor Hart, as they rose into the clouds.

V.R. Kaitlin hesitated, then continued to climb. "I'll circle until we understand what he wants," she told Trooper J.B. "If I abort now, we'll hit that cliff."

Trooper J.B. stared through the front window. A very hard, very solid-looking cliff was directly in front of them.

"Climb, Trooper Kaitlin, climb!" he shouted.

"Why?" Jeb shouted. "What's going on?" His voice was filled with panic.

V.R. Kaitlin pulled up and shot into the sky.

"Well," she said as they were circling. "That was interesting."

She glanced over her shoulder to see if Jeb was alive and well. He was alive all right, but she couldn't tell if he was well. He was sprawled out on the back seat with his nose face down. And his front paws were covering his ears.

"It's OK to come up now, Jeb," V.R. Kaitlin laughed.

Jeb opened one eye and looked out the window. When he saw that they were surrounded by clouds, he groaned and closed it again.

V.R. J.B. was attempting to contact the professor. "Sorry," he said, when he had established contact. "But waiting was a little, well, inconvenient."

"Yes, so I saw," the professor said.

"That's what I call a close call," Jeb moaned.

The professor explained his instructions. "I asked you to wait because you'll need a different vehicle. Bring the car back."

V.R. Kaitlin did as she was told. When she was on the ground, she stood beside V.R. J.B. and waited for the new vehicle to arrive.

Suddenly the Mothership appeared over the horizon.

"What is *that?*" Trooper J.B. muttered when he saw it.

"It's, well . . ." V.R. Kaitlin was practically speechless.

"The word's awesome!" Jeb said from the back seat. "I think I'll pass on this one. Catch me when it's all over." And with that, he lay back down on the back seat and closed his eyes.

"That is your vehicle," the professor explained.

Trooper Kaitlin and V.R. J.B. stared straight ahead as the Mothership moved closer.

"Am I supposed to fly that thing?" V.R. Kaitlin whispered.

"Yes, Kaitlin," replied the professor's voice. "And hurry, please."

Trooper J.B. and V.R. Kaitlin scurried into the Mothership. They made their way quickly through the vast corridors, until they reached the cockpit.

"This is unbelievable," V.R. J.B. said.

But V.R. Kaitlin wasn't listening. She was staring at the controls. "I'll never figure this thing out," she sighed.

"Remember that virtual reality video game you played a while ago, Trooper Kaitlin?" the professor asked.

"I remember."

"Well, this ship operates the same way."

"OK. I'm on my way."

As they rose into the sky, V.R. J.B. looked through the window and studied the scene below. V.R. Ryan was becoming a speck, and the silo was shrinking in size.

"What's that over there?" Trooper J.B. was trying to make out the objects below.

"I don't see anything." V.R. Kaitlin replied.

"Well, it's there. And I know who, or rather what, it is. It's Grimlord himself, and he's aiming his artillery gun right at us. We've got to destroy him."

"Don't forget about V.R. Ryan," Trooper J.B. said. "He's down there, and he needs a little time to locate the magician."

"There is no time," the professor reminded him. "Grimlord and the magician might put their plan into action."

"I must help V.R. Ryan now," the professor said. "In the meantime, I'm sending air support."

The Mothership dipped and buzzed the silo. There was no sign of V.R. Ryan, and there was no sign of the magician.

Suddenly the sky came alive with the sound of airships. V.R. Kaitlin pulled the nose up and joined them.

"Hold your fire!" she radioed. "V.R. Ryan's down there."

"There isn't time!" said one of the pilots. "Grimlord's ready to go. It might only be seconds before the world is destroyed."

"Just give him a few seconds," V.R. Kaitlin pleaded.

"We might not have a few seconds!"

Far below, V.R. Ryan was inspecting the silo.

"Do you see Grimlord?" the professor asked.

"Not yet," V.R. Ryan answered.

"He's to your left. In a second he will fire on our forces in the sky. You must stop him, and the magician, Trooper."

V.R. Ryan disappeared and reappeared behind Grimlord. In a second he had disarmed him.

"Where is my father?" he shouted.

"You will never see your father again." As the evil Grimlord spoke, a sinister little laugh echoed through the countryside.

"One, two, buckle my shoe," said the voice of the magician. "Three, four, tricks galore."

The magician laughed again and appeared beside V.R. Ryan. "I am the greatest magician in this world, and that world, and any world at all! I can make scarves disappear and pendants and . . ."

"How about fathers?"

"That too," The magician chuckled.

"We must get rid of that silo, Trooper Ryan!" instructed the voice of the professor.

"I'll be right with you, Professor," V.R. Ryan said.

Suddenly, he swung around and maneuvered a kick into the stomach of the evil Grimlord, sending him to the ground. Then without a second's hesitation, he took down the magician.

"Now lead me to my father," he demanded, as he held them down with his weapons.

"Gladly!" agreed Grimlord. "If you will just follow us, we will take you to him."

V.R. Ryan was about to go, but the voice of Professor Hart stopped him. "Don't do it, Trooper!" he said. "They will just take you prisoner, like they did your father. We need you. And please hurry. There is so much activity around there that we don't know what their plans are."

"What should I do?"

"Get away from those metalheads so that I can talk to you."

V.R. Ryan looked down at his father's jailers and sighed. It was no use. The professor was right. He wouldn't be any good to anyone if he was a prisoner too. He needed to be free to save his father, and the world.

V.R. Ryan reappeared beside the silo. "I'm ready, Professor," he said.

"We'll need to access some programs. We can do most of it from here."

V.R. Ryan waited for the professor's instructions. "Just gather some information and give it to us. And Ryan?"

"Yes, Professor."

"Please hurry."

V.R. Ryan worked fast, until he had related all the information that the professor needed.

And then he waited.

"Professor?" he asked, after a minute.

"Almost there," the professor said. "I think I've . . . yes . . . that's it."

V.R. J.B. and Trooper Kaitlin were waiting for instructions.

"Come in, Troopers," the professor said at last.

"What's going on?" V.R. Kaitlin asked.

"The world is safe. At least for now. But we still must do away with that silo."

"I've got the silo locked in," Trooper J.B. said.

"Instruct the backup airships to take care of the mutants."

"Hold your fire!" the professor said abruptly.

A few seconds later he was speaking to V.R. Ryan. "Remove yourself Trooper Ryan!" he instructed. "Immediately!"

Before he could issue another warning, V.R. Ryan was standing before him in the lab.

"Get ready to fire!" the professor instructed the airborne Troopers, when he was sure that Trooper Ryan was safely out of the way.

The Mothership proceeded toward the target and eased downward.

"Firing now!" Trooper J.B. reported.

A blast ripped through the silo.

"We have contact!" Kaitlin announced.

But the silo was still operational. Suddenly an explosion shook the Mothership and rocked Troopers J.B. and Kaitlin.

"Our weapons aren't powerful enough, Professor," Trooper J.B. said.

"You'll have to use the hypercannon," the professor answered.

"I'm on my way." V.R. J.B. leaned over and called for the hypercannon. "Cannon command!" he said.

The hypercannon came together.

"Power cells armed!"

V.R. J.B. aimed for the artillery silo and blasted away. A massive explosion shook the countryside.

"Direct hit!" Trooper J.B. reported. "No one will get any use out of that baby again."

"Good shot!" the professor said.

"And that," V.R. Kaitlin announced, "is the end of our good friend Mr. Grimlord."

"And our other good friend the magician," V.R. J.B. said.

The evil Grimlord was back on his throne—and he was seething.

"That silo took months to build," he said to the robot who stood before him. "And believe me, someone will pay for this. Ryan Steel will never see his father again. Now *be gone!*"

In a flash, the magician disappeared, and Grimlord was left alone to ponder the fate of Ryan Steel and his friends.

The magician reappeared beside the remains of the abandoned building. The world seemed strangely quiet.

And then he remembered the birds and animals. He waved his wand, and a butterfly came by. Birds sang, and rabbits scurried. The world was normal again.

"That's the end of that silo, Professor," V.R. J.B. reported from the cockpit of the Mothership. "Should we come in?"

"Let me check the target area," Professor Hart answered.

V.R. Kaitlin circled above the destruction as she awaited the professor's input.

"The building has been destroyed," he reported in a few minutes. "You can bring the ship down and return to the lab."

"What about Trooper Ryan?" Trooper J.B. asked.

"I'm right here," V.R. Ryan reported. "Is Jeb up there with you?"

"Negative!" V.R. J.B. answered. "We left him in the car."

Silence greeted him, as everyone thought about the car. Had it survived the onslaught?

Trooper Kaitlin landed the Mothership in record time. They couldn't get to the car fast enough. It was in one piece.

"*Ahhhhhh!*" Jeb was moaning, as they approached the car. "*Ahhhhhhh!* Make it stop! Please make it stop!"

"It's stopped, Jeb," V.R. Kaitlin assured him. "No more explosions."

138

"Oh yeah? That's what they all say. How do I know that magician doesn't have another trick up his sleeve?"

"We've destroyed him," Kaitlin promised. "He will never, ever bother you again."

But Jeb seemed skeptical. "I've heard all this before. Every time I'm feeling safe and sound, *Boom!* I'm behind bars or bombs are falling on my head."

Ryan was waiting for them on the other side of the portal. The three Troopers retroformed.

"How'd we do?" J.B. asked.

"I don't think those mutants will bother us again for a while," Ryan said.

J.B. and Kaitlin moved closer to the screen and looked up at the professor. "What about Grimlord?" J.B. asked.

"I don't think he could have survived that attack, but who knows. He's managed to elude us countless times before."

"And the magician?" Kaitlin said.

"We can only hope," the professor replied. "Oh, by the way, I've learned a little more about that land."

"You mean, Ziktor's wonderland of lush gardens and horseback riding trails? You mean Karl Ziktor's land of happy playgrounds for the children of our city?" Kaitlin laughed.

Professor Hart seemed confused. "I don't think so," he said after a minute. "I was referring to the land owned by the government."

"Don't mind Kaitlin, Professor," J.B. said. "What about it?"

"Well, I've been able to figure out where they keep the information. Perhaps I can help you access it, J.B."

J.B. hurried to the terminal and sat down.

"Type 'File 3004 admit.' "

J.B. did as he was told and shook his head. "No good, Professor."

"Then try '3004L admit.' "

J.B. typed it in and smiled as the information came up on the screen.

"This is high priority land," J.B. said. "They have no intention of ever selling it. In fact, they are worried that someone might sue if it turns out to be contaminated. But wait, it says that there are no signs of contamination."

"Well, that's a relief!" Jeb sighed.

Suddenly Kaitlin pulled a scarf out of her pocket and swung it around the lab. "Watch this," she said.

She stuffed the scarf into her fist. "Now you see it, now you don't."

Kaitlin opened her hand dramatically. The scarf was gone.

"Not bad, Kaitlin," J.B. said. "Not bad at all."

Kaitlin glanced over at Ryan to see his reaction. He smiled and nodded, but she could tell that he was thinking about something else. She knew what it was. Ryan was remembering the steaming coffee and the origami crane. He was thinking about his father.

"Not a bad trick at all," J.B. was saying. "But check this out. What we need is a little high-tech magic."

J.B. stepped up to the professor's materializer and placed a plate on it. "And now for the magic words," he said. "Sim, sim, sollabim."

J.B. punched a button and a hamburger appeared on the plate.

"HA!" Jeb said. "That was nothing! I've got a much better trick than that one."

"Really?" Kaitlin said.

"Sure. Put that plate down here where I can reach it."

J.B. took the plate from the materializer and placed it on the table beside Jeb.

"OK," he said. "Now everybody cover your eyes."

J.B. and Kaitlin looked at each other suspiciously. They knew what was coming, but neither of them said anything. They didn't want to ruin Jeb's trick.

"Now I'm going to make this hamburger disappear," Jeb announced.

Kaitlin and J.B. lowered their hands from their eyes and watched as Jeb devoured the hamburger. He wolfed it down quickly then turned and waited for their reaction.

"Nice try," J.B. laughed.

"Somehow, I saw that one coming," Kaitlin added.

Jeb smacked his lips and took a small bow. "What a dog has to do to get fed around here," he said.

On the other side of the lab, Ryan was beginning to smile.

"Good trick, Jeb," he said kindly.

"Thank you."

"But I've been thinking."

"About your father?" Kaitlin asked.

"About him, and about other things too. I've been thinking that tricks are really just illusions. And I've been thinking how fighting Grimlord has taught me the importance of knowing the difference between an illusion and reality. The hardest reality for me is knowing that, somewhere, my father is imprisoned, and that somehow I have to get him back."

J.B. crossed the lab and put his arm around his friend. "We'll find him, Ryan," he said. "If it's the last thing we do, we'll find him."